THE NAKED LIAR

WHAT SOME PEOPLE WON'T DO FOR A YOUNG WIDOW

The last time I'd been in a jewelry store I was drunk, armed with an empty .32 and filled with purpose; I had to collect money to help out the widow Craven. It didn't work out at all and I've hardly been interested in watches and rings since. This time I was cold sober, unarmed and uneasy. There was no reason in the world that Burkhardt would want to discuss handling hot goods and even if he couldn't resist the subject, I still wasn't convinced that Trixie hadn't done her Bernard in.

THE NAKED LIAR

HAROLD ADAMS
A CARL WILCOX MYSTERY

MYSTERIOUS PRESS

THE MYSTERIOUS PRESS • New York

The characters in this story are fictitious, and any resemblance between them and any living person is entirely coincidental

MYSTERIOUS PRESS EDITION

Mysterious Press books are published in association with Warner Books, Inc.
666 Fifth Avenue
New York, N.Y. 10103

W A Warner Communications Company

Printed in the United States of America

Originally published in hardcover by Mysterious Press
First Mysterious Press Paperback Printing: June, 1986

10 9 8 7 6 5 4 3 2 1

**To Barbara,
my favorite critic
and volunteer editor**

Chapter 1

The bugs came at dusk, black beetles about the size of a baby's thumbnail. They swarmed the northeast corner of the Wilcox Hotel up to the second floor, tumbled onto the sidewalk and crawled in all directions like animated ink. My nephew Hank took it all personally and was out on the walk trying to wash them away with hot water and a broom which he worked like a maniac. The bugs kept coming. They got under his collar, down his shirt back, and up his pant legs until he was busier than a rooster trying to screw two hens in a whirlpool.

Having lived through the dozens of bug invasions in South Dakota and the west, I knew there was no percentage in fighting them so I sat in the lobby, puffing a fresh-rolled cigarette and watched as Hank slaved and Ma egged him on. Ma will egg on anybody doing anything laborious however useless. She has a total passion for activity—any kind beats relaxing. Pa, who shares that passion when it's applied to anyone but himself, looked on in grinning approval.

The phone rang. Hank and his cheering section were too busy to notice so I ambled out to the hall, took the receiver down from the wall phone, and said, "Wilcox."

"Carl? How are you?"

"Worse," I said, trying to remember women I knew with husky voices.

"Ah, Carl, always kidding. Will you be serious a minute? I'm in a *really* bad fix."

"Oh?"

"I mean, having to call you like this."

"Why?"

"You *do* remember me, don't you?"

I finally did. "Sure, Trixie, you're Bernie Cook's sexy wife. What's on your mind?"

"Well, I'm in really serious trouble, Carl. You're probably the only fellow in the whole world who can help me."

The sensible response would've been, "Why me?" but I never took any prizes in that department so I puffed up a little and asked what was her problem.

"Well, I hate to tell you, it's so *embarrassing*."

"Maybe you'd better call somebody you know better."

"No, nobody but you can help. I can't talk about it over the telephone. Why don't you come to Aqua-town tonight—I'll explain everything."

"Where's Bernie?" I learned a long time ago you always make sure where the husband is.

"Well, actually, that's the problem. When you come, would you bring a good lawyer?"

That made me think a little. "What's wrong with Bernie's lawyer?"

"Oh, he won't help me at all. He thinks I did it."

"Did what?" I asked, knowing the answer.

"Murdered Bernard. It's all just too embarrassing and I've got to have help and you're the only person in the whole world who can save me. Carl! Please! You've got to!"

My God, I thought, another widow.

"I'm in jail, Carl," she pleaded. "I've never been in jail before and I'm scared to death and I know how clever you are and how you've helped other people and I always liked you, you were the nicest of all the fellows and the smartest. You *will* come, won't you?"

I thought about the bugs out front and the nuts inside and trying to stay sober in Corden on a Saturday night. What the hell, how could it be worse?

"Okay," I said. "Take it easy and give me about an hour or so. I might have some trouble coming up with a lawyer tonight, but I'll try."

"Oh, Carl, I just knew you'd save me! You're such a Galahad!"

No, I didn't swallow all of that whole, but I enjoyed it and of course was promptly locked into trying to prove it was all absolutely true. So I called Howie, a fledgling lawyer without enough money to court ladies, let alone marry. He spent his evenings at the boardinghouse where he was looked after by his old-maid landlady, Carrie Olson.

"A rich widow in Aquatown needs a good lawyer," I told him.

"Really?" I suppose he was suspicious because the last time I got him a client it was Boswell, my bootlegger friend, who'd tried to pay him off with moonshine. Of course, Howie doesn't drink.

"Uh-huh. This one can pay off with things better than moonshine."

3

"That's encouraging," he said doubtfully. "Who is she?"

"Mrs. Bernard Cook. Her man's been murdered. The cops like her for it and she's hollering for help. I convinced her you'd be just the ticket."

"My God. You and widows. This one's husband isn't cold and you're already involved. Or was it the husband? You said 'her man.'"

"Yeah, it was the husband, and don't sound so disrespectful, Howie. Lawyers get rich by being professionally respectful. You want to come along and spring her tonight?"

"Tonight?" He squeaked with indignation.

"If the cops keep this lady overnight, they may never want to let her go. She's quite a dish."

He stewed over that a few seconds and then asked, "Did her husband really have money?"

"Does Eddie Cantor have daughters?" I usually try to avoid flat-out lies.

He turned suspicious. "So he must have had his own lawyer. What about him?"

"I think he hopes the lady'll get nailed and he'll have a free crack at the estate."

"You mean he thinks she killed him and won't take the case."

I sighed. "That's what she told me."

"Great."

"She can pay, win or lose. She wears enough rocks on her fingers to buy a good lawyer even at hockshop rates."

He thought about it awhile. "How close friends have you two been?"

"You know me, I got nothing but close friends. Come on, do it or get off the pot, okay?"

"I don't like it. She's got to be awfully desperate if she has to turn to you for help."

"Okay, if you're so damn rich you don't need clients, say so and I'll try to find a real lawyer."

"Don't get huffy, I'll take her. Come over and pick me up."

Ten minutes later we were wheeling along the graveled highway toward Aquatown in my Model-T coupe while I filled him in on Bernard Cook. I didn't tell him I'd always called the man Barnyard because he was so full of shit. People said that when it came to liars you had the plain ones, then there were damned liars, next Goddamned liars, and finally there was Bernie Cook. He couldn't tell you the truth about the weather if you were standing beside him in a rainstorm.

What I did tell Howie was that Bernie had brought Trixie back from an eastern trip about four years ago. I believed that because *she'd* told me so. He'd been a salesman all his life. He peddled vacuum cleaners, snake oil, spot removers, Bibles, condoms, and booze. I even suspected he'd made some money on Trixie and wouldn't have been surprised to hear he knew the price of his mother before she died. You get so you'll believe anything about a guy like Bernie except what he tells you.

"I haven't seen much of them lately," I told Howie, "but I used to play pool with him and took in a few of his poker sessions at the house. He ran regular games Friday night ever since I first knew him."

I'd won my share of the pool games, but he had a good edge in poker because knowing him I couldn't believe he didn't bluff more often than he actually did. Of course that was the double-liar's technique.

"What's the wife's first name?" yelled Howie over the motor and the wind.

"Trixie."

"My God."

"You know her?" I asked, turning to look at him.

"Watch the road. No, I don't know her. The name's enough."

He was silent until we reached the city limits and then asked where I'd met her.

"At his house. Friday night poker session. They welcomed strays. After a while, when I'd find the table full, I'd hang around and kid with her. She was always there, bringing drinks and sandwiches. Bernie called her his good luck charm. The guys claimed he kept her around to make them forget their hands."

"How'd she feel about that?"

"Mostly she didn't mind. She'd laugh and kid 'em along."

"Ever see her get mad?"

"Oh, sure. Then she'd smoulder. I never saw her throw things or yell much."

"A real lady," he said.

"Not exactly. Although I doubt she'd lay down with anybody unless Bernie okayed the price."

He turned to stare at me. "Did you ever pay him to lay down with her?"

"Nope."

"Oh, you thought you could manage without paying, I suppose. Or didn't you like her looks?"

"There's nothing wrong with her looks. She's got a great shape and she's full of fire."

"So what held you back?"

"Never had the money."

He thought that over for a few seconds while he watched ahead, then turned to me again. "You wouldn't buy her," he said, "because you don't approve of a man selling his wife."

I laughed.

He nodded his head. "I know, it's not the money, it's the principle. I'm beginning to get you figured out. You're full of principles, you just don't understand them because you reject God. You reject everything your parents accept."

We'd arrived at the police station by then and I parked, cut the engine and waved him out. "Stick to law, Howie, you don't know shit about religion or principles."

He gave me a smug look and got out.

Sergeant Wendtworth was at his desk in front and gave me his picket-fence grin. There was a little more red in his face and gray in his hair since I'd seen him last, but his husky voice and broad bottom hadn't changed. He whistled up a young cop who led us down the wide, creaking hall. Trixie wasn't in the rear cell block; they'd put her in a small interrogation room with an army cot so she could have privacy not available to the common prisoners. Prostitutes went into ordinary cells on the rare occasions when one was collared, and they were about the only women ever arrested in Aquatown.

At first glance, Trixie didn't quite fit my build-up. She was red-faced with anger and her hair straggled around her neck in blonde curls. Her blue eyes blazed.

"Look at this!" she demanded, waving her glittering hands. "I'm supposed to sleep on a cot and when I want to go to the john I've got to ask permission and they take me where all the cops go. Is that any way to treat a lady?"

"Would you rather have an open cell where all the rummies could gawk while you used the can?" I asked.

That shocked her pale and speechless, but not for long.

"What a thing to say! Whose side are you on—?" Suddenly she noticed Howie and after a split second's hesitation she figured out he was the guy who might get her out of jail. Her hands went to her hair and she smiled radiantly. "Well, Carl, aren't you going to introduce me to this gentleman?"

I did and when he offered to shake she grabbed his hand with both of hers.

"I'm really delighted that you came," she cooed, pulling him toward the cot. "Here, sit beside me, and please forgive my rudeness. I'm so terribly upset and distraught I'm simply not myself. Are you from the cities?"

"Uh, Corden," said Howie, blushing.

"Oh, of course. That's all right, dear, I'm sure you can help me. You look ever so intelligent and capable and I'm sure Carl has confidence in you and that's good enough for me. Can we go now?"

"Well, uh, not just yet—"

"How silly of me, you've just arrived, haven't you? And so kind to give up your evening and come to help me. I'm *so* grateful. You want to go talk to the people and arrange things now?"

I butted in. "He wants to get acquainted with his client first, Trixie. He's not positive he wants the case."

She drew back a little but didn't let go of his hand. "You're not sure?" She gave him all the blue eyes had and it was enough to make him wilt.

"I, uh, just want to be sure I can help you . . . ."

She gave me an imploring look. "Didn't you tell him I couldn't possibly have done it?"

"What I think isn't what counts," I told her.

She looked back at him and blinked her eyes, trying to pump a tear or two.

"Mrs. Cook," said Howie, "why don't you just tell me what happened, starting from the beginning?"

She gazed at him soulfully for a moment, then released his hot hand, smoothed her green skirt over her knees, and crossed her ankles demurely.

"Bernard had his usual Friday night poker game with the usual fellows and I'd made sandwiches and brought drinks and of course they had all been smoking cigars and cigarettes so there was this terrific mess to clean up after and I stayed downstairs to do it while Bernard went up to bed. I wasn't feeling sleepy even after all the cleaning up so I sat down and read a magazine while I had a cup of coffee."

"Was that your normal pattern?" asked Howie.

"Huh?"

"Did your husband normally go to bed ahead of you?"

"What do you mean, normally?"

"I mean, did that happen other Friday nights?"

"What difference does that make?"

Howie's brow wrinkled earnestly. "Mrs. Cook, on this night your husband was murdered. That made it a very un-normal night, didn't it? So I have to find out everything that made this night unlike others."

"Well, I don't see—"

"Trixie," I said, "for God's sake, answer the man's questions or we'll be here all night."

She gave me a dagger look, touched her hair absently with one hand and finally sighed. "So okay. It wasn't normal. I was mad at him and I didn't want to go up till I was sure he was asleep. You know why."

"You'd had a fight?" asked Howie, looking worried.

"No! I never fight in public. But I wanted some

respect and when the guys were around he always treated me like a bum waitress. It was, 'Trixie, where's the grub?' and 'Trixie, for God's sake, get us another drink.' And when I wasn't running around fetching he wanted me to sit close, bending over so guys would try to stare down my front and forget about the poker game. It was embarrassing. They were wise to that and only gawked when they'd dropped out."

"Did you have words about this in front of the fellows?" asked Howie.

She shook her head, making her curls bounce.

"Remember, Mrs. Cook—"

"Call me Trixie," she said, giving him a load of her dimples.

"Uh, yeah. I was saying, remember that the police will be talking with everyone in the game that night. Be sure what you remember is going to be what *they* remember."

The dimples vanished. "Nobody remembers anything the same, that's silly. So maybe one or two of the boys noticed I wasn't too gay. I didn't holler or throw things the way most women treated that way would. I was a lady and nobody can say different."

Howie wiped his forehead. "Of course you're right, I just want to avoid any surprises; you understand, don't you?"

She softened, smiled and leaned his way. "Sure, go on."

"Okay, so when everyone had left, you read some. Do you remember what it was?"

"*Liberty* magazine."

"Then what time did you go upstairs?"

"About three, I guess."

"All right, what did you do?"

"Well, I went up and peeked into the bedroom and

saw Bernard all spread-eagled on his back, naked as a jaybird and with the pillow over his face. I figured he was clowning so I didn't even go take the pillow off. He was always doing crazy things like that to fool me, so I decided the hell with him and went to bed in the guest room. That's what the cops won't believe, that I left him there with the pillow over his face, but he was breathing when I saw him. How was I to know he'd die under it?"

"Had he vomited?" I asked.

"How'd I know? Nobody told me anything. All they keep saying is, it looks very funny and nobody ever suffocated from just having a pillow over his face and they say he couldn't have tied the knots himself, they were too tight. The trouble is, none of these people knew him, what a liar he was. You know, don't you Carl?"

Howie turned to me with his mouth open, unable to follow her line of reasoning and I didn't figure it'd help to try any explanations.

"He was very tricky," I assured her.

"Well, I'll say so. That's not the half of it."

Howie shook his head like a groggy fighter, turned back to her, swallowed and said, "Then what?"

"I went to bed and slept till there was this pounding at the front door. I hollered at Bernard, but of course he didn't answer so I put on my robe and went down and there was this cop saying they'd had a call about trouble at our house. I got mad and said that was crazy and he asked where was my husband and I told him in bed and right then I started getting scared because everything was so weird. I didn't want the cop to come in before I could check on Bernard, but he was a pushy bastard and I couldn't stop him. He just went upstairs and found Bernard as I'd seen him the last time only he looked gray and awful. The cop walked over, jerked the pillow away, looked at me and went back down to use the telephone. I went crazy for a while—I kept hollering that Bernard was a liar, not dead at all—it was another trick, another lie. Jesus, I was really crazy, but who wouldn't be in a fix like that, I ask you?"

"Was the house locked?" asked Howie.

"Locked? No, we never locked anything. Who locks around here?"

"Were you drunk when you went to bed?" I asked.

"Carl, you know me, I'm no lush."

"What time did the cop show up?" asked Howie.

"Oh God, I don't know—it seemed like I'd just shut my eyes but it was light out. Probably six or so."

"Had Bernard ever done that sort of trick before— I mean, like tying himself up?" asked Howie.

"He'd never tied himself up before, but he was always pulling some damned idiotic stunt. He came home once with his arm in a sling and another time he had some cretin friend put a cast on his leg. Sat around in the easy chair a day and a half, letting me think he was an invalid and waiting on him hand and foot—"

Howie watched her face with his boyish blue eyes wide and bright, his forehead wrinkled. His gaze never dropped below her throat and I realized he was afraid of her body. I remembered his attitude of a year before when we'd been in one of the back cells in the same station, questioning old Boswell. Then Howie had stood in a corner, listening impatiently while I asked all the questions. Now he sat close and showed impatience only when I stuck my oar in.

Trixie fascinated, awed, and frightened him. She

was probably the first grown woman he'd ever met who wasn't a carryover Victorian.

Despite this, or maybe because of it, he could see she was holding out on us. She didn't want to go into any more details than she'd spilled in the first runthrough. He didn't have any luck in drawing out details on her marriage and finally sat silent, watching her. She straightened up, arching her body and putting her hands on her lower back. When she smiled at him, for a moment he just stared, then a foolish grin spread across his young face.

"You're going to help me, aren't you?" she said.

"Of course." He turned sober all at once and even frowned.

"Tell me, Mrs. Cook—"

"Call me Trixie."

"Uh, yes—considering the fact that Mr. Cook exploited you and was inconsiderate, why'd you stay with him?"

She arched her eyebrows. "We were married. I promised."

Chapter 2

Lieutenant Baker beamed when Howie and I entered his office and even stood up to shake hands. He looked bigger than ever with his black hair slicked back, tight as a paint job and parted so true it might have been done with a cleaver. Thick-lensed glasses hid his eyes, but his smile said he was happy. I'd been lots more comfortable when he'd been mean and natural.

"You work long hours," I said.

"Always on Saturdays, especially this one."

"I'd like to know," said Howie, "how the policeman happened to go to Cook's house this morning."

"Simple. We got an anonymous call, saying somebody'd been killed there."

"Did this caller claim he heard Cook being smothered?" I asked.

"No, he didn't. Could be he'd heard Cook yelling when Trixie was working him over with the riding crop."

Howie's mouth sagged. Mine probably did too.

"He was striped like a zebra," said Baker cheerfully. "All over the chest, belly, and thighs. A real working over."

Howie closed his mouth, blinked, and looked at me.

"What does Trixie say about that?" I asked.

He smiled sweetly. "Doesn't know a thing about it. Says she never heard a sound. In case you're interested, her prints are on the crop handle. Nice and clear."

His smugness over the case made Baker as accommodating as a madam on Monday and he gave us names of the five guys who'd been in Bernie's last poker game. Four were regulars, the fifth a stranger. I wrote down their addresses because Howie was too stunned to function and then walked him outside where we stood in the warm evening breeze.

Howie remained in a daze while I rolled and lit a cigarette. The flare of my match seemed to bring him around; he looked back at the station, took a deep breath and said, "I guess I'd better go back and talk with her."

"Sleep on it," I said. "I'll take you back home."

He shook his head. "I don't want her thinking I've abandoned her."

"You're going to take the case?"

"Of course. It's obvious she's been framed." He glared at me. "You see that, don't you?"

"Oh, sure," I lied.

"I'll get her side of it. You wait here. I won't be long."

He was reasonably honest about that. I only got through two more cigarettes before he popped out looking a touch frazzled but resolute.

"This is going to be a tough case," he said.

15

That was encouraging. The last one we were on together he'd called hopeless and we came out fine.

In the car he admitted that Trixie was properly grateful but seemed to lose faith when she realized he couldn't spring her at once. When he asked how anyone could have beaten Bernard without her hearing, she said it was because she'd had the radio on loud.

"While reading?" I asked.

"She explained that she always had it on loud so she could hear it all over the house."

"So how'd she account for her prints on the quirt?"

"She said she'd handled it—they just fooled around with it. She swears she never hit him."

People like Howie are what makes it possible to believe faith can move mountains. At least it can for people like him.

"Okay," I said. "Tomorrow I'll see the guys who were at the game. Maybe we can get something to work on from them."

"Maybe I'd ought to come along."

"Uh-uh. A lawyer just naturally makes people clam up. Let me do the snooping, you do the lawyering."

"Well, okay, but I'll come back with you. I should talk some more with Trixie."

"You plan to talk with her all afternoon?"

"Well, no."

"Because I've got five guys to talk with—and it could be more if they give me any leads."

"Don't worry, I'll find something to do."

I assured him I wouldn't worry a blamed bit, I just wanted to be certain he knew how it was going to be. He was silent the rest of the way home. I think he was looking forward to a long warm talk with Trixie.

Chapter 3

                                                    Joe   Johanson
lived on the north side in a dinky bungalow with a
worn lawn and two dried-up lilac bushes flanking
the walk. The house needed paint and the porch
steps sagged. My knock was answered by Mrs.
Johanson, who listened with interest and watched
me with dark eyes as I explained who I was and why
I wanted to talk with Joe. It was plain the idea of
murder excited her silly and she was ecstatic at the
notion of getting inside information. She invited me
in, yelled down the hall for Joe, and said she'd bring
coffee while I made myself comfy.

The shades were drawn over the living room
windows leaving the dark furniture half hidden in
shadows. A reddish-brown, home-braided carpet
filled the room's center. I eased into an easy chair in
the corner which I figured was Joe's. A moment later
he came down the hall from the bathroom where I
could hear the flush action in full voice. For just a

second he peered at me in the gloom and then his head lifted slightly and he said, "Carl?"

He was tall and hunched, like a man made lintel-shy by too many cracks on the head through adolescence. Thick hair tumbled across his wide forehead and his blue eyes were separated by a hooked nose that would have done credit to a pirate captain but looked only clownish over his clean, slightly receding chin.

I said hi, got up to shake and he edged me away from his chair and settled back as I took the corner seat of the matching couch.

I told him why I'd come and he scowled.

"I told the cops all I know. I don't know what the hell you think you can dig up."

"I won't know till I try, Joe. You still throwing sand in a cement mixer?"

"Naw, I'm foreman of the crew now."

"That's great."

"As long as it lasts. Which could be less than a week longer."

He was bitter and cold. I asked about the job he was on and he told me without satisfaction or pride. Just as I was ready to try steering talk to the last Friday night poker game, his wife came in bearing a coffee tray. We helped ourselves to cups, she poured and we used cream and sugar and spoons.

I watched Joe's plump, dark wife. She was quick and perky as a wren and her bright eyes stayed on me hopefully, as if she felt positive I was going to make the dull day exciting.

"What's your theory, Mr. Wilcox?" she asked. "Who do you think killed Bernie?"

"I don't know, I haven't even read the newspaper stories."

"Well, you must've talked with the police. You said you were investigating—"

"Yeah, but they don't tell me much. Have you got any ideas about it?"

"You bet I have."

"Oh, God," said Joe.

"The wife did it," she said.

"What the hell do you know?" demanded Joe.

"I know what I've heard, and not just from you, either. And I've seen her. She's a brazen hussy with bleached hair and floozy clothes."

"Why don't you just hush up and let Carl ask the questions he came here for?"

She settled back, holding her cup with both hands. "I thought I'd save him some time. Besides, he asked if I had any ideas."

Before he could yap back I butted in and asked how he thought Trixie and Bernie got along.

He quit glaring at his wife, shrugged and said he guessed they got along about like most couples.

"You mean they scrapped a lot?"

That brought his beak up. He gave me a dirty look and said he and his wife got along fine.

"So how'd they compare with you two?"

"They scrapped lots more."

"Did they scrap Friday night?"

"Not exactly. Things were a little chilly. I came in kind of late and it seemed like maybe I'd missed something—I never knew what."

"So what went on that made you think that?"

"Well, Trixie was in a pout and she went upstairs early."

"Who else was there when you got in?"

"Big Tiny, Ike, Gene, and a new fella."

"Podolack?"

"Yeah, I guess so."

"Anybody beside Trixie seem upset?"

"I guess Big Tiny was, a little. You know how he is about Trixie. If she ain't happy, he ain't."

"What about Bernie. How'd he act?"

"Crazy, like usual. He was on this stranger, kidding him a lot, you know how he does."

"How'd the stranger take that?"

"Dead pan."

"Did he have eyes for Trixie before she went upstairs?"

"Yeah, you could say that. When old Bernie laughed about her barging off, he said something I didn't catch and for a second there, Bernie stopped grinning. He made some kind of comeback and this guy looked a little surprised but not much. I don't think there was anything to it."

"You think this guy Podolack might've thought Trixie was for sale?"

"How the hell'd I know? He had eyes for her, that's all I know."

"Did you think she was interested in him at all?"

"Naw, she never looked at him."

I asked him about the relationship between Trixie and the other poker regulars. He told me to ask them and said it in a tone that suggested any more questions in that line would cut off the dialogue. Remembering that he'd always had a sense of humor like a gila monster, I gave up the notion of kidding him into a better mood and when I'd finished my coffee, thanked them both for their time and left.

Gene Healey was the youngest of the poker crowd; a curly-haired, smooth-faced kid with teeth so white and neat they'd have looked phony except for one on the upper right that was a shade catty-wampus. He played what he considered a percentage game and it drove him nuts when Bernie seemed to win regularly on luck. He wasn't quite as stupid as that makes him sound but he wasn't the brightest light in South Dakota either. I found him at home in his dinky downtown apartment.

He acted real pleased to see me, invited me in, apologized for the messiness of his place, wailed politely about Bernie's death and asked a little too casually how I'd happened to drop around.

I explained.

He said, "Ah."

I asked what that meant. He looked innocent.

"You think she killed him?" I asked.

"Don't you?"

"You think I'd try to help her if she did?"

He laughed. "Sure, if she asked."

Obviously he had no higher regard for my intelligence than I did for his.

"Okay, assuming you're right, what do you figure made her decide to do it that night instead of any other time in the last four years?"

"Don't get me wrong," he said earnestly, "I don't blame her at all. Old Bernie's been asking for it."

"So what happened special Friday night?"

"Just the same old stuff." He laughed again. It was like a hiccup. "I lost. Everybody but Bernie lost. There was this new guy there, giving Trixie the eye, and Bernie was egging him on and trying to get Trixie to bend over to give him an eyeful. She was wearing this green kimono that was really the cat's meow, I *mean*."

I'd been missing something, apparently. In my day she'd stuck with low-cut blouses and tight skirts.

"Since when had she been wearing a kimono?"

"That was the first time, I think."

"Joe told me he thought something had happened

before he showed up that got people in a stir. Did you see anything?"

"I only got there a little before him but I noticed the same thing. The only guy in the crowd having any fun was old Bernie. I thought he'd got drunk a little early. And he did seem to be pushing something with this new guy. It was all kind of weird, actually."

He couldn't, or wouldn't, get more specific about that. I asked how much did he figure he'd lost to Bernie in four years?

"Oh, lordy, don't make me think about it. I must've *averaged* five to ten bucks a week. Course I didn't play every week."

No, I guessed, not losing half his pay. Selling clothes at Schuman's wasn't exactly like panning gold in the Klondike. I remembered times when Bernie had raised the ante and said that was to get the shoe clerks out. About the third time he pulled that, Gene had flushed and said he didn't sell shoes. Bernie gave him his look of injured innocence and assured him that was just an old poker playing remark, like "down and dirty" or "play, said the losers." It was just chatter, didn't mean a thing. He didn't mention that the object was to make losers mad and reckless. That was the kind of game Bernie ran. Real poker players don't play to make friends.

"Did you ever get ideas about Trixie?" I asked.

He tried to look shocked. "What kind of ideas?"

"Come on, Gene, we're big boys now."

He laughed, sobered and looked away. "I had dreams about her a couple times. Didn't we all?"

"Did she ever flirt with you?"

"Well, sort of. You know how she is. But not like she did with Big Tiny. I think that was because old Bernie would never figure Big Tiny'd get anyplace, you know? But if she was to flirt with me, it might mean something, me being younger and all."

"Did she flirt strong with Ike?"

"Not strong. He didn't react much. That's another reason she worked on Tiny, she could always make him blush. She got a big kick out of that."

"Did she flirt with this new guy, Podolack?"

He shook his head. "She never looked his way. She didn't like him at all."

"Any notion why?"

"Well, not really. It might've been because Bernie seemed to be pushing her his way. Bernie had a mean streak that way, you know. He seemed to get a bang out of making her mad. He'd just push and push once he had her sore. It always made Ike mad as hell because he thought it slowed the game down. Ike liked to stick with poker."

"Did you think Big Tiny was upset?"

"Oh, sure. He always got upset when Bernie made Trixie mad. He'd say, 'Hey Bernie, come on, be yourself.' It'd have been funny if it wasn't so sad. Old Bernie *was* being himself, that was him all over."

"Did you think Trixie liked you?"

"Sure. Lots of times, when I'd lost a big pot, she'd come around and pat my shoulder. And times when I dropped out broke, she brought me a drink and talked to me."

"You never thought that maybe she was put up to that by Bernie so you'd keep coming around to play?"

"No, not at all. In fact, sometimes Bernie'd look our way when we were apart from the poker table, and he'd scowl at her. He didn't mind when she did that with Ike or Joe or Big Tiny. You know?"

"You think that night was a last straw, that she just got fed up and finally killed him?"

He hitched around almost as bad as a fresh-mounted bronc in a rodeo stall and shook his curly head.

"I don't figure she did it on purpose. It probably happened more by accident. It must have. Who else could have done it with her right there in the house?"

"That's the problem," I admitted.

"Maybe she can get by on self-defense?"

"Not when he was the one tied down to the bed."

"He could've threatened—"

"Who'd believe a threat from the biggest liar in the state?"

He gave up and shook his head.

I leaned toward him. "Just between us old poker pals, Gene, was there ever a time when you'd like to have knocked him off yourself?"

He brightened up at the thought. "Man, I used to dream of it. Only I never thought of using a pillow. I'd rather used an axe."

Chapter 4

Ike Olson's house was bigger than Johanson's, with a fair-sized lawn browned by the summer sun. Elms lined the southern edge and shaded the house through hot afternoons.

I knocked on the front door and heard him holler for his daughter Adair to answer but she didn't show and pretty soon he came mumbling to the porch.

Ike stood five-four and carried his head thrust forward like a hungry hawk. Gray, bristling hair framed his ears and left his crown bare and gleaming. His brow jutted as fiercely as his jaw and gray eyebrows hid his sharp blue eyes when he lowered his head, which was often. The eyes were like ground owls, deep in their burrows, peering out full of threat and rage. Somehow he always had a half-finished stogie in his mug.

"Never know where that damned kid is," he grumbled, "What the hell are you doing here? Trixie talk you into helping her out?"

"You been looking in a crystal ball?" I asked as he shoved the screen open and let me in.

"Huh!" he said, leading me to the living room. "Who needs one? When a damned fool woman kills her man the first thing she'd think of was finding another man damn fool enough to bail her out. You show up and I got the answers. You sure as hell didn't come around for old time's sake."

"I guess you aren't too crazy about Trixie."

He sank into a morris chair, leaned back and took the cigar from his tight lips.

"Like hell. She's a damned fool, killing him that way. Why didn't she just poison him like any sensible woman would?"

"Maybe she didn't have a supply handy at the moment. I wouldn't guess she's one for long-range plans."

"You can bet your ass on that. She can see about as far ahead as a goat."

He shoved the cigar back in his mouth and massaged the chair arms with his bony hands. The fabric had been worn almost as bald as his crown. I sat across from him on a sagging couch which wasn't quite as abused as the chair and looked over the brown and gold Persian carpet which sat dead center in the parlor exposing wide stretches of handsomely varnished hardwood floor.

"You mad because you think she killed him, or because you think she didn't do it smart?"

"I'm not mad at her, and I don't blame her for doing the job. God knows he had it coming."

"And it's hard to be mad at a good-looking woman, huh?"

"Not if she's a birdbrain."

"You don't like that in a woman?"

"Sometimes it's handy, but mostly it drives me

nuts. Only birds ought to have bird brains. Did you come here to ask me did I kill Bernie or did you just want to ask cute questions until I solved the whole thing for you?"

"Whatever'll give me the whole story."

"You got the whole story. No, I didn't kill him. She did. She had the reasons, the chance, and to my surprise, the guts."

"That was a big surprise?"

"Hell, yes. If she'd had real spine, she'd have killed him four years ago."

"So how come, all of a sudden, she changed?"

"The old last straw, that's all."

He took the cigar from his mouth and examined it. It wasn't lit or even chewed that I could notice. It hardly looked wet.

"If he was so hard to take, how come you played poker with him every week?"

"I wanted to beat his ass. We weren't buddies, we were enemies. That's what poker's about. Who wants to skin his friends?" He stuck the cigar back in his face and scowled.

"What kept Trixie and Bernie together?" I asked.

"They were two of a kind. Abusers, apologizers, forgivers—all that. He'd rag her ass all day, she'd beat his at night, they'd forgive each other in the morning and start all over. Never happy unless they were miserable. Crazies, two of a kind, perfect goddamned match."

"What do you mean, she beat him at night?"

"What the hell do you think I mean? She pounded him with the riding crop. He'd let her tie him up and whale the daylights out of him. The madder he made her during the day, the harder she'd pound him at night. Then she'd untie him and they'd go at it."

"Did he tell you that?"

"Yeah, and I believed him because he showed me the welts. He couldn't lie about them, I'll tell you."

For the first time since I'd arrived he didn't look fierce, he looked satisfied.

"So what happened Friday night that made her put the pillow over his head and sit on it?"

"Who the hell knows? Maybe it was because he showed Podolack her snatch."

"He what?"

"She came by, carrying drinks and old Bernie grabbed her kimono, flipped it open and said, 'Look at that! You ever see an honest-to-God blonde before?' And then he went on to say blonde stuff is better than any other. I thought that Polack's eyes'd pop out of his head."

"What'd Trixie do?"

"She jerked loose and moved on like nothing happened, but her face was like a beet. I figured right then, by God, she'd cut him in half with the old quirt before the night was over."

"Who was there when this happened?"

"Just old fat Tiny. That poor bastard, he nearly swallowed his tongue. He's had it hanging out for her so long it's a wonder he hasn't stepped on it."

"Was he mad?"

"That big slob? He doesn't get mad. He'd more likely bawl, but he didn't even do that. He just turned purple." He shook his head in disgust.

I thought about it all for a while and finally asked if everybody'd left at the same time.

"Naw. Joe and I took off first. It was a lousy game and everybody was owly as hell but that damned fool Bernie. He was riding this Podolack, Tiny was in a sulk, Trixie took off, Joe gloomed around as usual—he's another one with his tongue hanging out for Trixie. It was all disgusting."

"So Gene Healey, Big Tiny and this guy Podolack were still around when you left? Were they still playing poker?"

"Naw. Just jawing and boozing."

"What makes you so sure only Trixie could've killed him?"

"Who else would he have let tie him up? How could any of those guys have smothered him with Trixie right there? And who'd have framed Trixie? All those guys were panting for her."

"You're sure of that?"

"Positive. Who the hell could hate *her*?"

Yeah, who?

29

Chapter 5

Big Tiny Sorenson was the biggest man I ever met. Folks claimed it'd take a grain elevator scale to weigh him, and he stood just under six-and-a-half-feet tall, walked with an elephant's sway and was so muscle-bound his arms didn't swing, they just flopped on his sides. He couldn't touch his pants seams without bending his elbows. His pumpkin head smile stretched so wide it about dimpled his earlobes and his crinkled eyes closed when he laughed.

His landlady told me I'd find him at the Cozy Café and there he was, polishing off a slab of apple pie with about a pint of ice cream. He'd just finished two orders of hot pork sandwiches and four side dishes of creamed corn. I sat across from him and ordered a cup of coffee from a slim waitress who was looking a mite peaked from hauling all the groceries to Big Tiny's table. His big smile of greeting faded to a sorrowful droop when I explained why I'd come.

"Trixie never did it," he said, waving his fork

earnestly, "at least, not on purpose. That poor girl's gonna shrivel up and just fade away without Bernie, you wait and see. They'll never hang her, she'll pine away first."

They don't hang people in South Dakota, but I decided this wasn't a time for making fine points. "You say not on purpose. You think maybe she was mad enough to do it by accident?"

He got so flustered he dropped the fork which bounced from the table to the floor. There was a flurry as the waitress trotted over to give him a clean one and fumbled under his chair for the one he'd dropped.

I repeated my question.

"I don't believe she killed him anyway. Trixie's not that kind of a girl."

"I hear Bernie flipped her kimono open for Podolack's benefit. You ever see him do anything like that before?"

Tiny regarded his pie and ice cream for a moment, put his fork down and shoved the plate away. "Not that I remember, no."

"Did you get the idea that Bernie was planning a little sale?"

He turned red and shook his head. I expected it would shimmy like a bowl of jelly, but only his jowls shook.

"You ever see him try to sell her before?"

"Never." He didn't try shaking his head again. I stared at him and felt lousy about it because he seemed so damned vulnerable. His eyes went back to the rejected plate, he reached out with his massive paw, pulled it back and slowly began eating again.

"How long have you known Trixie?" I asked.

"A long time. Even before Bernie."

That startled me because I'd heard she came from the East, but he explained they'd both been with a carnival; she danced in a girlie show, he'd been the barker. Before that he'd done a strong man act that flopped because his fat hid his muscle and nobody believed the stunts. He'd met Bernie while the show was in Minneapolis and had introduced the couple.

"Trixie always said I was the fattest cupid in history," he said, giving me his pumpkin grin.

I asked how she'd liked doing a girlie show and he said it had been fine for a while. She liked showing off her figure and exciting guys, and while she wasn't a great dancer or quite as vulgar as most of the others, she'd been real popular. When the show went East in the fall, Bernie followed along, got her to quit and married her. Tiny had returned to South Dakota a few weeks later and they'd stayed friends.

"Tell me about Friday night," I said.

"I don't remember anything special." He'd finished his dessert and was drinking sugared coffee.

"Except for the kimono flipping deal."

He didn't want to talk about that. I asked him if he knew about the whipping routine Trixie and Bernie practiced in their bedroom. He turned red so I suspected he did, but he denied it and he told me, very reproachfully, that I hadn't ought to talk about the dead like that. He turned his head away, looking around as if hoping to see a friendly face that'd end this line of talk.

"Look, Tiny," I said. "I'm not just digging for gossip or trying to make your friends look bad. I'm just after any facts that can help me sort this business out and I can't be squeamish about any of it."

He gave up looking for a friend and met my eyes. "If she beat him," he said softly, "it was because he

32

wanted her to. He knew he was bad to her and wanted her to punish him because then she'd forgive him. He couldn't help being the way he was, a liar and a nasty man—"

"How about a cheat?"

He nodded sadly. "She understood him and she did what she did because he wanted her to and she loved him. You can't tell me anything about Trixie, Carl. I know her better than anybody, no matter who you talked to. And she didn't beat him to death, they say he was smothered. She couldn't do that by accident."

"Okay, I agree with that. So help me figure out how to find proof that somebody else did. That's all I'm after."

He swallowed hard, looked away and his eyes got watery but didn't spill.

"How about this Podolack guy," I said. "Did he hang around after you decided to go?"

"No. I think he wanted to, but Trixie had gone upstairs and Bernie turned sour so he left with Gene and me. Outside the house we went different ways."

"Talk any before you split up?"

"No. None of us felt like talking, it wasn't a friendly night."

I asked him to tell me about Podolack and got only a massive shrug.

"How'd he act toward Bernie?"

"Watchful. Like he didn't trust him."

"How about Trixie?"

"He watched her too, hungry-like."

"How'd she react to him?"

"Paid him no attention. I bet she couldn't tell you what he looked like if she had to."

"How'd he learn about the party?"

"Well," he said, looking uncomfortable, "he came

33

into Fino's when I was there and we got talking and I must've mentioned the game and he asked could he come along so of course I said yes."

I asked who'd started the conversation at Fino's and he wasn't sure. He couldn't remember who'd steered the talk but admitted that while Podolack hadn't said much of anything about himself, he'd done pretty well at digging out stuff about Tiny and his crowd. I asked when the party broke up. He said a little after one A.M.

He asked did I think I'd be able to help Trixie and I said I wasn't sure.

"Keep talking to her friends," he urged me. "They'll tell you she didn't do it."

The trouble was, so far it looked like he was the only friend she had.

Chapter 6

I don't know whether it was the brown suit, the wide cheeks or the fact I was expecting to see Podolack that made me guess it was him when he came out the front door of the boardinghouse as I strolled up the walk. He topped me by about half a head and gave me a quick once-over before I spoke.

"Your name Podolack?" I asked.

"Don't tell me," he said, "you've been checking mug books."

"My name's Wilcox. I'd like to talk about Friday night at Bernie's."

"I wouldn't," he said, and brushed by me. I caught up and walked by his right side. His stride forced me to hustle, which makes me irritable.

"What're you afraid of?" I asked.

He gave me a casual grin. "Not you."

"So you're brave. You figure the lady killed her husband?"

"What's the difference what I think? I'm a stranger in town, I don't know from nothing."

"It might make a lot of difference. All the other guys at that party were regulars, they probably didn't pay much attention to what was going on. But a stranger, who kept his eyes open and had some smarts, he might notice things."

"What's it to you?" he asked, looking down at me. "You're no cop."

"That's right," I said. "I'm in the mug book with you."

His head turned and he took me in for a couple strides, then grinned. His teeth were a little brown but nice and even, the jaw was big and squared.

"You got the look," he told me, and turned in at a candy and tobacco store. A moment later he came out opening a package of Old Golds. He didn't offer me one but stood still after getting a cigarette in his mouth and lighting it. His pale hands were as thick and smooth-skinned as his face.

"I'm a friend of the family," I said, "trying to help out."

"Ah," he said. "Hot for the widow."

Since he no longer had me trotting like a terrier my irritability had dropped and I let his crack pass.

"If you were a stranger, how come Bernie was expecting you?"

His head jerked my way and his eyes narrowed. "Where'd you get that notion?"

"He had Trixie dressed special. He sure wouldn't do that for the regular crowd."

"Maybe he liked the kimono himself. It looked pretty good."

"Especially when he flipped it open for you."

He grinned, exhaled smoke, and looked across the

street at the lower branches of a box elder. I built a smoke of my own.

"Did you know about that poker game before you met Big Tiny at Fino's?"

"Nope."

"So Tiny invited you to the game."

"That's right."

"And you met Tiny for the first time at the bar after dinner?"

"Isn't that what he told you?"

"I just wanted to be sure."

"Uh-huh. You know, you're persistent as a fly on a hound's nose. You think anybody'd give a damn if I just flattened you?"

"You bet. Kids'd be coming around for your autograph, if you survived."

He liked that. He even laughed. It was more like a short bark, but I knew it was a laugh because the corners of his mouth went up.

He started across the street toward the park and I trailed along. We sat down on the first bench.

"Okay," he said. "It was a nutty night. Yeah, the guy showed me what she had, she didn't like it, I thought it was fine and nothing came of it."

"You figured he was pushing her at you?"

"Hell, yes, who wouldn't? I thought he was a pimp. Tiny'd said she was his wife, but I couldn't believe any guy'd push his wife. I asked that old fart, the little guy—Ike?—if this guy was selling the woman and he said he probably would if the price was right."

"You make an offer?"

"Naw, she huffed off upstairs. It was plain she wasn't in the mood."

"Did that make you mad?"

He grinned. "Just made me sore."

I didn't have to ask where. "What'd you do when you left Bernie's?"

"Found me a whorehouse."

"Which one?"

"The cops know."

"That doesn't help me."

"It was on the south side, Fourth Street, I think. Upstairs."

"Big Nose Nellie's, right?"

"I didn't see any sign."

"With a nose like Nellie's, who needs a sign?" He leaned forward, resting his elbows on his knees and gave me a sideways look. "You been there?"

"I've been everywhere. What brought you to Aquatown?"

"I heard they had natural blondes."

"You mean you were looking for Trixie?"

He looked disgusted. "That was a joke, pal."

"I figured it was supposed to be, but you're a deep guy, I thought maybe you were trying to tell me something."

He shook his head wearily, dropped his cigarette butt and watched it smoke slowly in the dust.

"What was it you said to Bernie when his wife went upstairs?" I asked.

He turned his brown eyes my way and looked at me as if I were a mongrel that had suddenly said, "Hi."

"I asked him," he said slowly, "where was the toilet. He gave me a long look and said I'd find one downtown."

"What'd you make of that?"

"I figured he was nuts. He'd been throwing her at me all night and all of a sudden he makes like the jealous husband."

"It didn't dawn on you they were battling and you'd been used?"

His big jaw tightened. "Yeah, I thought of that later."

"You didn't mosey back after the others left, just to talk it over with him, did you?"

He sat back, relaxed, smiled and shook his head. "Come on, do I look like a guy who'd go crazy over a piece of fluff like that?"

"You look like a proud man."

"Proud, hell. I'd never lose my head over a piece of tail. Would you?"

"Been doing it all my life."

"You must've killed a lot of guys."

"There've been a few casualties. Had you ever met Big Tiny before you happened on each other in the speakeasy?"

"No."

"Who started the conversation?"

"He did."

That figured. Tiny was a natural gabber and too big for anyone to ignore. "What'd he tell you about the Cooks before you went over to their house?"

"He said there'd be a poker game."

"He say anything about the natural blonde?"

He took out his Old Golds, shook one loose, stuck it in his face and lit it.

"Yeah, he talked about her."

He leaned back again and I turned to face him. His ear was small and hairy, tight against his smooth skull.

"He sounded like a proud husband," Podolack went on, "bragging about his wife. And at the house, even after she turned snotty, she still managed to kid with him. You could tell he was the only guy in the place she thought was okay."

39

"You said 'after she turned snotty.' Was she in a good mood when you first got there?"

"Well, she didn't start off snarling."

"So what changed her? The kimono flip?"

He exhaled smoke and frowned thoughtfully. "No, that was just the final straw like. It'd been building up." He grinned and glanced my way. "I think she started to burn because her old man was making noises like maybe she and I could get together."

He looked across the street and scowled. After a moment I asked if he thought Tiny'd ever made out with her.

"Sure as hell not on top. She'd be flatter than a steamrollered turd if he had."

He worked hard to make that sound funny, but I knew it riled him to think Tiny might've managed to make out where he couldn't.

"I guess you were pretty sore at both Cooks before that evening was over."

He gave me a long scowl, glanced around the park, stood up and moved in front of me, glaring down.

"Listen good, Shorty. I left that poker game and went to a whorehouse. Then I went back to the boardinghouse and slept all night. Now I'm sick of you and your ugly puss and your goddamned questions. Don't come around again. Don't go talking to the cops about me. You do and I'll break your back. You understand?"

"Sure," I said, and smiled. Then I uncrossed my legs so quick he jumped back, thinking I was going to kick, and the next moment I was on my feet with my nose close to his chin.

"We'll see each other again," I told him, "and there's one thing you'd better understand."

"Yeah?"

"Nobody ever calls me short more than once."

For a second he stared, then he laughed, shook his head and walked off.

Chapter 7

Howie had the mankind-loving look of a convert fresh from church when I picked him up a little after four at the police station. He asked politely if I'd learned anything from the poker players but was too excited by his afternoon with the lady to show any concern when I said no. I asked what he got from Trixie.

He took a deep breath while pulling in his chin, and launched into it.

"Do you know why she married Bernard Cook?" he asked.

"He was a good-looking stud with a line that made her dizzy."

"She thought he needed her," he corrected me. "She saw his lying as something he did because he was so unsure of himself."

"Girls always go for the shy ones."

He smiled at me tolerantly so I'd know that sarcasm was wasted on this sublime subject.

"She was confident that with her help, he could

make the most of himself, and she was honest with me, she wanted to get away from the carnival life and she knew there wasn't much of anything else she could do but wait on tables or something equally menial. She's too sensitive for that sort of thing."

"Sure."

"He was a very aggressive suitor, you know. He gave her three different engagement rings, each one bigger than the last. They showed her he was serious and, of course, generous."

I didn't ask what he'd given her lately.

"She's very domestic," he said proudly. "She knits. Sweaters and sox and things. And she likes to cook. Did you know you roast pheasant in milk? And you can make cupcakes and cookies with sour milk?"

I guessed he was the only man in South Dakota ignorant of those facts, but when I nodded he didn't notice. He told me she also read a great deal and did her own hair.

"She's never been to a beauty parlor in her life."

I tried to look impressed but it didn't matter. He was gazing off into dreamy space somewhere just beyond the radiator cap.

"Now what're you doing?" asked my old man, Elihu, when I arrived at the hotel after dumping the moonstruck Howie at his boardinghouse.

The old man was parked in his wooden swivel chair, elbows on the arms, heels on the windowsill, smoking a La Fendrich which he rolled gently between long, tobacco-stained fingers.

"I've been promoting a blonde in Aquatown," I said.

"From here?"

"Well, she's in jail so I couldn't spend the evening with her."

His bright blue eyes took on a fogged look through

his uncleaned glasses. "I suppose she's the one who murdered her husband?"

"The cops think so."

He took a drag on the cigar, blew out small smoke rings and raised one hand to touch his fine gray hair. "And now you're gonna find out who really done it and save her, huh?"

"I keep telling you, don't read the last chapter first."

He ignored that. "I suppose you're doing it all for love."

"Yup, and any money that might come along if she's cleared and inherits."

"Oh, you're planning to marry for money?"

"You got a better reason?"

"Not for you."

He doesn't hate me for any real personal reason. Mostly I think he blames God for wishing me on him because he sure as hell won't acknowledge any blame for how I turned out. Also he resents me because I'm from the wrong generation. Ma, on the other hand, considers me punishment for her sins. They don't fight over their differences because I just naturally pull them together against the common foe. Me.

Nephew Hank came around to interrupt the warm dialogue and asked all about the murder, so I filled him in. I said I figured the killer had to be the guy who hated Trixie because she'd been framed so tight. He'd wanted to get her more than Bernie.

"Are you kidding?" he asked.

I said sure, but I wasn't because it never pays not to kid. If you're proved wrong you never pretended to be right and if you're right they assume you meant it.

"I guess this is another case where you won't get paid."

"Well, I'm used to that."

After a dinner of lamp chops, my least favorite meal this side of goat meat, I ambled down the street to the railroad tracks and dropped in on Boswell.

His shack, which he built from boxcar lumber, has catty-wampus windows facing the tracks and is filled with cast-off furniture, old magazines, newspapers, cardboard boxes loaded with dusty bottles, rusting tools, twine, rope, wire and rags. He's never thrown anything away and dotes on stuff others discard by their garbage cans. No nail is too old, bent or rusty; everything has an eventual use if you plan to live forever.

He was cleaning supper dishes in the sink and turned to give me his vague smile as I stopped in front of his easy chair in which was curled Patsy, his black-and-white rat terrier. She opened one brown eye and peered at me.

"Move," I said.

She wagged her stump tail.

"Patsy!" I said, louder this time.

She opened both eyes and wagged her whole rear end. I kept staring and finally she lifted her head, gave me a disapproving look and hopped down.

"It's easier," said Boswell, "just to pick her up and move her. She doesn't mind that. You want some coffee?"

"If you put a stick in it."

He poured a mug three-quarters full, topped it off with a shot of moon from a can on the shelf under the sink and brought it over to me. After we'd lit smokes and settled back, Patsy hopped in his lap, making him spill a little coffee, which he ignored, and he asked how was my ma and pa.

"Intolerable."

"That's nice."

"Why do you ask how they are? They've been out of the hospital four years now."

"It was a bad accident."

"It wasn't an accident, and anyway, they came out okay."

"They're pretty old."

"They aren't as old as you are."

"Well, that's pretty old."

We smoked and drank coffee for a while.

"You ever know a guy named Bernie Cook, in Aquatown?" I asked.

"Seems like," he said, after a moment.

"Tall, fast-talking dude, world's biggest liar. Got a wife named Trixie."

"Uh-huh. Pretty."

"He ever buy your moonshine?"

"Once."

"Only once?"

He nodded.

"I see. He never paid for it, right?"

"I suppose he forgot."

"That bastard never forgot anything."

"You ain't supposed to speak ill of the dead," he told me gently.

"So you heard."

"Uh-huh. Trixie never done it."

"How'd you know that?"

"I know."

"You say stuff like that as if you're apologizing when all you're really doing is being bullheaded. Why can't you ever give a reason for your opinions?"

"I don't have reasons, I got feelings."

"You're as bad as Howie. Only his feeling is lust."

"Well, he's a young man," he said, as if that

explained everything. After some thought, I decided it probably did.

"The trouble is, Lieutenant Baker's positive she did it."

"Uh-huh. That's the fella figured I killed Miz Bonney."

"I'm not so sure he did after the first day. He just held you in case he couldn't find the real killer. With you in the pokey he figured folks'd think he was doing something useful."

Boswell puffed serenely on his stinking pipe and patted Patsy.

"There were five guys at the game Friday night," I said. "They all knew Trixie was mad at Bernie, at least a couple of the players knew Trixie and Bernie did weird things—they'd fight and then she'd whip him and it was all cozy as bull-baiting. He was smothered with a pillow on the bed while tied to the posts, spread-eagled like a pelt on a wall."

Boswell shook his head sadly. "I hope he was drunk."

"He might have been, but he never hit the jug as hard as he let on to the poker crowd. You can't win regularly with a bag on."

"He won regular?"

"Yup. Always knew when to fold."

"That the secret?"

"It's the most important one."

Someone passed the window to the right of the door I was facing and appeared beyond the screen, peering in.

"Come on in, Howie," I said.

He pulled the screen open, stepped inside and stared around the cluttered room looking offended.

"I thought you'd be here," he said accusingly as he stared at my cup.

Boswell moved Patsy from his lap to the floor, stood up, offered him his chair and asked if he'd like coffee. Howie accepted to be polite, but from his expression I knew he didn't plan to touch his clean lips with anything in that shack. After delivering unspiked coffee, Boswell put the pot back on the stove and parked on a wooden box.

"So what's on your mind?" I asked.

"You didn't really tell me about your talks with the poker people," he said. "I thought if I got the details, maybe I could make something of it all."

I stared at him so long he got nervous and absent-mindedly sipped the coffee and looked surprised when he found it was okay. He drank some more to be sure and relaxed a little.

"I should tell you," he said, "Trixie's very grateful, but she's frightened. She swears she never beat Bernie at all."

"Uh-huh. Let me tell you something, Howie. The first thing you'd better get straight is that this woman knows you're hot for her and she's not going to tell you a damned thing she thinks might scare you off. And until she admits she worked her hubby over with a quirt that night, she's lying. Nobody used that thing wearing gloves without smearing or wiping out her prints. She beat the hell out of him. She wanted to and he wanted her to and don't you forget it."

He glared at me, drank some more coffee and stared into the mug as he lowered it.

"She's had a hard life, you know. Orphaned when she was eight, grew up in foster homes, was arrested once for running away—"

"She told me she'd never been in jail before."

"Well, she probably wasn't in a cell. Look, Carl, I

know she's not a saint, but she didn't kill her husband. I *know* that."

"Yeah, you and Boswell. Okay, we'll do our damnedest to prove you're both right; now, let's go home and get some sleep."

Chapter 8

Tuesday I drove back to Aquatown, entered the police station and spotted a blonde sitting on the waiting bench in the hall leading to the cells. At first glance I wondered what the hell Trixie was doing out there. Then I realized this one was wearing quiet clothes. Trixie was strictly a primary color girl, mostly red and green. This one wore black, a suitlike affair with white ruffles at the collar and cuffs; almost school-girl proper.

"Who's the frail?" I asked Sergeant Wendtland.

"Trixie's kid sister, from the East. Go tell her who you are, she'll probably fall all over you."

"What's her name?"

"Rita Gates."

"Married?"

"No ring."

I walked back and stopped in front of her. She looked up.

South Dakota is maybe the blue-eyed capital of

the world, but this girl had them so bright, clear and wide they put all the rest to shame. I didn't notice until later that her cheeks were faintly pocked and she wore a thin layer of powder over faint dabs of rouge. Her lashes were black and long under neatly painted brows, the pouting lips were bright red above a firm round chin. She blinked slowly, like the movement of a butterfly when it's sitting on a flower and opens its wings.

"I'm Carl Wilcox, the guy your sister called for help. She asked me to get a lawyer and try to find out who killed her husband."

She gave me another slow blink, said how do you do in a low voice and invited me to sit down. I accepted. She turned her body to face me and stared into my eyes with an expression that hinted she was hoping to find something better inside than showed on the surface.

"Are you old friends?" she asked.

"Not real old. It's just that I know some people and have been involved in a couple things—"

I was interrupted by Baker, who came out of Trixie's room down the hall and waved Rita his way. She excused herself, rose smoothly to her feet and a moment later glided through the door down the hall. Baker ambled over to me.

"Some quail, huh?" he leered.

"Don't start planning to shoot her down."

"Wouldn't dream of it. I leave that stuff to you."

"Has Howie been in?"

"Has the sun come up? He'd have breakfast with her if we let him. You got a moonstruck buddy there, Wilcox, he'll never do her any good. Gone gaga."

"Don't sell him short, Lieutenant, he's a smart boy."

"He's a lovesick calf."

"Where's he now?"

"Probably out looking for his private eye, expecting a miracle. You got one handy yet?"

"Before long," I lied cheerfully.

"Bullshit," he said, and went back in his office.

Rita came out looking grim after about twenty minutes with Trixie. I got up, asked if we could talk a little and she gave me another look that started with hope and ended with resignation.

"Why not? Is there a decent place around here for breakfast?"

I took her west to the Cozy Café and found a booth near the back. Our fat waitress was fascinated by Rita—probably took her for a strayed movie actress—and carefully wrote down her order for poached eggs on toast, orange juice and coffee, plus bacon. She bustled off and returned at once with coffee for us. Rita thanked her and the waitress blushed with pleasure, waved the coffeepot and drifted off.

"I'd guess you're some younger than Trixie," I said.

She sipped the coffee, set her cup down, gave me an eyebrow glance and said, "You're a detective, all right."

I remembered Ma's remark once that sarcasm didn't become a lady. I guessed this one could get away with it.

"About ten years, I'd guess, between you."

She gave me a more respectful glance. "That's right."

"Trixie told us she was orphaned at eight."

She grinned, sipped coffee and laughed when she put her cup back in the saucer. "What's that make me? An afterbirth?"

"What's the facts about your parents?"

"What's that got to do with murder in the far West?"

"This isn't the far West, it's not even halfway. What I'm trying to find out is about Trixie."

"You've got your work cut out for you," she said and smiled at the waddling waitress who marched up with breakfast. I waited until everything was set down, the waitress was gone, and Rita tied into the food. She didn't exactly attack it, but the way she stabbed the yolk was enough to make me expect it to splatter, and for a few seconds I just watched in awe as the whole business on her plate did a disappearing act.

"I guess you don't want to talk about family," I said.

"Ma lives in a walk-up in Newark. God knows where Pa is, and nobody cares."

"He left you all?"

"Flat."

That wasn't quite accurate considering the shape of the daughters, but I let it pass and asked when he'd left. She finished her coffee and looked up for the waitress, who rushed over and filled her cup. I got no attention, not even a refill, until I called the waitress back. She apologized but didn't look at me.

"The way I remember hearing," said Rita, "was that Pa left right after dinner. If he didn't appreciate anything else, he dearly loved pork roast, mashed potatoes, and gravy. He ate it all, mopped the plate, and went for a stroll at six-thirty on a Friday night in July. It was the tenth, nineteen-fourteen. I was four."

"And you remember all that?"

"No, but Trixie does. She's talked about it all our lives. Took it personally, as if he left because of *her*.

Oh, she blamed Ma, of course, but never believed she really mattered. Trixie always thought if she'd handled things right herself, Pa'd have stayed around no matter what else."

"Did you know Cook before Trixie married him?"

"No, I met him at the wedding. They had it in New Jersey so Ma could come and Trixie could show off her pretty boy. I figured him for a phony right off—all that big talk and the glad eye. All Ma said was that he was certainly a fine-looking man. She thought all men looked fine."

"Is that why your old man left her?"

"Could be. Not because she was fooling around, but because she didn't think he was anything greater than any other guy. Men think they've got to be the greatest thing in the world to their women."

"Women think different?"

"Sure."

"You think Trixie could've knocked off Bernie?"

"Of course not. She's a born sufferer."

"Did she tell you who she thought might've done it?"

Her pouty mouth grimaced. "Anybody. She thinks they'd all have killed him to get at her. She just won't believe anybody tried to frame her. She thinks that just happened."

"Well, how'd you like to think somebody'd tried to frame you for murder?"

"I wouldn't like it, but I wouldn't be stupid enough to ignore the facts."

No, the little sister wasn't a girl with illusions. She asked me what I was doing about the case and I told her.

"You figure it was one of the poker crowd?"

"I'm not taking it for granted. Other guys that

played poker other times would know what went on most nights."

"Guys like you?"

"Nobody's like me."

Her dark eyebrows lifted a fraction and she smiled like someone close, welcoming you as you got off a train. "Okay, but do you have an alibi for Friday night?"

"Yup. I was in Corden, minding the hotel while Ma and Pa were playing bridge at the Wilkersons'."

She looked me over, still smiling, steady and cool. "Why'd Trixie think to call you? Have you been to bed with her?"

"Never."

She sighed. "Maybe that's the reason. You've got good eyes, at least. Have you really solved a killing or two?"

I nodded and she shook her head. "I can't quite picture it."

"I don't look much like Charlie Chan," I admitted.

Her smile got wider than ever. "You're not thin-skinned, are you? Okay, what do you do when you're not detecting?"

"Whatever's handy. Jackknife carpentry, sign and house painting. Drove a truck until it died and I didn't have the heart to buy another."

"You mean you didn't have the money."

"Isn't that what I said?"

She pushed her plate away, put her elbows on the table and cupped her chin with her hands. "You're really kind of a bum, aren't you?"

"That's right. What're you?"

"Me? I'm sure not in the home repair and touch-up business."

"What do you do?"

"I'm an entertainer."

"Song and dance?"

"More or less. Anyway, I'm no suspect in this case—I was a thousand miles away."

I offered to roll her a smoke and she shook her head.

"Gives a girl bad breath."

She watched as I rolled my cigarette. I got the notion she was strangely interested in the black hair on the back of my hands which gives them the look of paws.

"What nationality are you?" she asked.

"Irish, English, Scotch, and French. Strong on the black Irish."

"I guess you've got hair on your shoulders."

"Everywhere, Rita, except the palms and bottoms of my feet."

"Let me see," she said, and reached for my hand. I let her take it and she stared into the palm. "You've got a long life line," she told me, "but the love line is a mess."

"Am I going to be rich?"

"No. But now and then you'll be comfortable. You'll travel a lot. You always have, haven't you?" I nodded. She peered into the hand. "You've been married, haven't you?"

"Uh-huh."

"But it didn't last at all. And you've been involved with a widow. My goodness—more than one, I think. But you won't marry one." She frowned and shook her head. "There are an awful lot of women in your life."

"Clear to the end?"

"It looks that way." She glanced up at my face, apparently finding some trouble in making my kisser match up with the palm record.

"You can't figure out how I manage, huh?" I said.

"Do you know?"

"Sincerity, I guess."

"No. You're all recklessness and romance, almost a pirate except you're not really ruthless. You're warm and loyal and at the same time very dangerous. I've never seen a weirder palm in my life."

"I bet you tell that to all the boys."

She turned my hand over, slapped it and sat back. "You don't believe there's anything to palm reading, do you?"

"I figure it's about as reliable as crystal balls, goat innards, and prayer."

"Men always pretend to be skeptical, but they love having their palms read."

"They just want you to hold their hands."

"They'd rather tickle my palm."

"I can sure believe that."

She met my gaze. Suddenly there was a whole new relationship between us. I'm not sure whether she'd decided I was an interesting character, or that maybe I could be useful, but for the first time she took me seriously.

When the waitress returned I asked for the bill and paid her. Out on the bright street the wind blew hot and dry. Rita hesitated on the walk, trying to get her bearings, then squinted at me.

"You really think you can help Trixie?"

"That's pretty much up to her. I think she's holding back and they've got a hell of a case against her. She's got to make me believe she didn't do it before I can get anywhere."

She began walking east and I moved with her.

"Take my word for it," she said, bobbing her head for emphasis, "Trixie didn't smother him. She admits she beat him, he wanted her to, he liked it, but she was so damned mad at him afterwards she didn't let him loose. She just walked out. Somebody went in there and did the pillow job."

"So why didn't she tell the police that?"

"Oh, hell, she's ashamed to tell those guys Bernie liked whippings, or that she humored him. She figures they'll think she's a pervert."

"She'd rather have them think she murdered him?"

"They already think that. Believing she was a pervert would just make it that much easier for them to see her as a murderess."

"Uh-huh, but as the Norse Nightingale says, 'When lie ban fulish, tal the truth.' When those guys catch you in one lie, they don't believe you ever tell the truth."

We walked between the pillars of the Compton Hotel which tries to look like a southern mansion, and entered the high-ceilinged cool, lobby. Rita walked to a big couch against the north wall and sank into it.

"Tell you what," she said as I plunked down beside her. "What if I guarantee you you'll get paid for your efforts to help her, whether Trixie's proven guilty or not?"

For some reason it embarrasses me to talk about money with women and I tried to wave off the notion that I'd even think of such a deal, but she got a determined look and leaned close.

"I'll give you a check for two hundred dollars as a retainer, okay? What do you charge a day?"

If a man asked I'd have said ten or twelve, depending on how flush I figured he was, but with her I couldn't imagine such a thing.

"How about five?" I said.

"Who'd do anything tough for five dollars a day? I'll give you eight. If you have expenses, I'll cover them. Booze isn't what I consider an expense in this case."

"You got a lot of money?"

"I've got enough and I know where to get more. Don't worry, my check's good. And if that worries you, I'll make it cash."

"Look, I can't guarantee you anything."

"You promise me you'll do your best—I'll settle for that."

"Lady, you're crazy. You just met me. You know I'm an ex-con?"

She grinned. "I've read your palm, I know you better than anybody but your mother—and maybe better than her. You'll do the job if it's possible."

"Come on, that palm stuff is hokum."

"What do you care as long as I'm satisfied. I'll get cash for you."

She stood up, hiked over to the hotel cashier and had a conference. A moment later she was back.

"Come back in an hour. I'll have the money then."

I got up and when she stuck her hand out I took it.

"We'll shake on it, okay?" she said. Her blue eyes were wide with excitement and she looked like a high school kid accepting a date for the junior prom.

Chapter 9

Howie refused to believe Rita's report that Trixie admitted beating Bernie. I found myself trying to explain that this didn't mean she was sadistic, she'd just been screwed up because she loved the damned fool and wanted to please him. Even while I was making this pitch I wondered if I'd been twisted myself by prospects of money from the little sister. Since when, for God's sake, did I try to justify other people's quirks to anybody for any reason?

He asked what else she'd told me and I explained she was guaranteeing my fee.

His eyes narrowed suspiciously. "Where's her money come from? She got a husband?"

"No. She says she's an entertainer."

"A *what*?"

"Entertainer. Doesn't she look like one to you?"

"The trouble with you," he said loftily, "is that you believe anything a good-looking woman tells you."

"Don't we all?" I said, and decided not to tell him Trixie wasn't an orphan. "Let's go see Trixie."

"There's no need for you to go along."

"Yeah, I think there is. I'm the only one who's been paid in advance."

He didn't like that but wasn't up to debating the point, and half an hour later we were in her room at police headquarters. I let Howie lead off and he hemmed and hawed around so long I thought we'd overstay visiting hours before he got any answers. At first she was outraged when he explained why the police were so positive she'd pounded Bernie and then she turned humiliated and at last admitted it, "but only because he'd been so hateful all that goddamned evening and I was too mad not to do it and anyway he'd worked it all out on purpose. He always did even though he knew very well I wasn't a girl like that."

She worked herself up beautifully and cried with her face covered and didn't leak enough to wet a gnat's whisker. Howie put his hand on her bowed shoulder and offered his clean, white linen handkerchief which she wrinkled up into dirty laundry in five seconds.

"Trixie," he said, "didn't your husband have business dealings with men besides poker players? Wasn't he involved with criminals from the cities?"

So Howie wasn't moonstruck to the point of blindness after all; he'd been doing some checking on his own. Trixie lowered her hands, lifted her head and stared at him.

"You think Bernard was a crook?"

"That's not the question," he said firmly. "The question is, did *you* know he was and who did he deal with?"

"Well!" she said, and gave me a dirty look.

"I've been told," said Howie, "that Bernard sold stolen goods. Quite a lot in the last two years."

Trixie turned her blue eyes from me to him, wiped her dry cheek with the linen and gazed past us dreamily.

"He sold some second-hand things. Costume jewelry, a few clothes . . ."

"Last month he sold a stolen Cadillac to a man out at Lake Kampie."

"I don't believe that," she said with dignity. "And if it's so, I don't know anything about it."

"Where did he buy the jewelry you're wearing?"

"From jewelry stores, right here in town." She jerked her head so her curls bounced, and looked down at her glittering fingers.

"Which stores?"

She let him know by her drooping mouth and hurt expression that he was treating a nice girl in a cruel fashion. He believed her but had convinced himself that to save her he'd have to be ruthless and he was, by God, going to ruthless her to death if that was the only way to manage it.

So we left with the names of two jewelers and I set out to talk with them.

Chapter 10

The last time I'd been in a jewelry store I was drunk, armed with an empty .32 and filled with purpose; I had to collect money to help out the widow Craven. It didn't work out at all and I've hardly been interested in watches and rings since. This time I was cold sober, unarmed and uneasy. There was no reason in this world that Burkhardt would want to discuss handling hot goods and even if he couldn't resist the subject, I still wasn't convinced that Trixie hadn't done her Bernard in.

Burkhardt's place was designed to discourage sneak thieves. As you entered the front door you passed between glassed partitions that screened off the watch repairman's bench to the right and a squat safe on the left. Beyond the partitions, large glass cases on legs lined a wide aisle and beyond the clerk's walk there were glass cabinets displaying watches, clocks, and knickknacks. Toward the back there were display cases filled with delicate china and silverware, silver platters, coffee urns, creamers, sugar bowls, and a million things that'd make Ma's mouth water. But there wasn't an item you could touch without someone handed it over.

Under the balcony over the extreme rear section which looked dark under its low ceiling, a man sat at a desk in the gloom. A gooseneck lamp lit the desk top, leaving the man's face in shadow.

"May I help you?" asked a voice to my right.

The watchmaker had left his bench and stood behind the nearest case, looking at me as if he figured I was going to ask for a handout. He was young, already losing his hair and putting on weight. His suit was dark, his shirt white, the vest puckered. His navy blue tie had daringly wide stripes. A touch of the rebel. A very light touch.

"I want to talk with Burkhardt," I said.

"*Mr.* Burkhardt's busy just now. Would you like to tell me what you want to see him about?"

"It's personal," I said.

He smiled sweetly. "Is it personal personal, or business personal?"

"Maybe a little of both." I glanced toward the back of the store. The man there ignored us.

"If it's to do with business, you can talk with me. Mr. Burkhardt resents interruptions when he's working on the books. You wouldn't find him very easy to talk to just now."

I rested one elbow on the glass counter and glanced down at the rings in their velvet-lined cases.

"You people buy second-hand jewelry?"

"It would depend."

"On what?"

"The quality. The risk."

I glanced up at him. His face had the innocence of a jowly rabbit. His clear eyes met mine directly.

"What do you mean, 'risk'?"

"We wouldn't want to buy anything where there might be some question of legal ownership."

"You mean hot goods?"

His smile remained innocent. "That's right."

"What kind of proof would you need?"

"A complete identification of the customer, perhaps some references?"

"I see. You only buy hot goods from people you know."

"We only buy second-hand goods from people we can find later if it becomes necessary," he said, still smiling.

"Uh-huh. Like a guy named Bernard Cook."

The smile faded a little. He looked back at the boss, gave me a curt nod and said, "Would you mind waiting here a moment?"

I said why not, and he hiked briskly off. The man at the desk didn't lift his head until the watch repairman had spoken several words, then he turned and looked at me. A moment later the watch repairman waved me back to join them.

Mr. Burkhardt didn't get up or offer to shake hands. He just told his hired man to go back up front. Then he tilted his swivel chair back for a better view of me and I took in his sad, seamed face. He looked at least eighty years old and from his expression, he'd suffered every day of it, not from pain so much as disillusionment and loss.

"Why are you asking about Bernard Cook?" he asked.

"I hear he sold some things for you now and then."

"I hire no salesmen. I have a shop, people come in. On busy days, which are rare except before Christmas, my wife comes to give a hand. When I go to lunch, Kenny takes care of things. Why would I need a salesman?"

"Maybe I heard wrong. Maybe he sold things *to* you."

"Never."

"So how come the mention of his name suddenly made your boy think you should talk to me?"

His mouth twitched; I guess it was as close as he ever got to a smile.

"Mr. Cook had a certain reputation. And he did offer me goods once or twice, at rather suspiciously low prices."

"But you didn't buy?"

"In the jewelry business, sir, in a town of this size, reputation is everything. One simply doesn't deal with people like Mr. Cook and expect to stay in business."

"You know his wife, Trixie?"

"I know her by sight. She came in with Mr. Cook, who bought her some things. Costume jewelry and silver, mostly."

"That was before he offered you the bargain goods, eh?"

He nodded.

"Do you know if he dealt with any other jeweler in town?"

"I do not."

I jerked my head toward the front of the store. "How about Kenny? Could he have handled any deals on the side while you were out to lunch?"

"Certainly not. The idea is laughable."

"Why don't you laugh, then?"

"It's too preposterous," he said. "Good day, sir."

* * *

Neither the safe nor the watch repairman's bench were in public view at Hadas' Jewelry Store. A young woman, smartly dressed and made up bright as a Christmas doll, greeted me from behind the first display case and asked if she could help. I'd planned to ask right off if they bought used jewelry, but the lady was so classy I couldn't manage to think of an opener and she looked suspiciously on while I gulped a couple times.

"Well, maybe," I finally said. "What I'm looking for is something old-fashioned, I mean, sort of an instant heirloom, you know?"

"Is this for an older woman?"

"No, a younger one, almost as young as you, but she likes things that've been around, like me."

She didn't smile. "What did you have in mind? A ring? A brooch?"

"A brooch, maybe."

We moved on to the next display case and she took out one tray at a time while I examined stuff that ranged from the impossible to the incredible. All the time she watched me, trying to decide whether I was casing the joint for a heist or was some eccentric millionaire.

"Do you people ever handle any used pieces?" I asked, after we'd gone through everything she thought would fill the bill and she'd carefully put all the trays out of reach.

"Occasionally Mr. Hadas picks up things from estate sales. Just now I don't know of anything. You might try Burkhardt's."

"He buys second-hand stuff?"

She looked haughty. "None of us are pawn shops."

I smiled but the frost didn't melt. I hadn't shown enough interest in the right things. "Okay, is Mr. Hadas in? I'd like to talk with him."

Her eyes opened a little wider, and then she went over to a wall case, put her finger against something out of sight and kept her eyes on me.

Hadas was dark, quick, and calculating. My first thought was that a man so young couldn't own a shop like this honestly unless he'd inherited it. His height was about the same as mine, his black suit made him look small but I guessed he outweighed me by fifteen pounds. He walked with a snapping stride to within three feet of me and halted. On the approach he had appraised me from dusty toe to tousled crown and I'd been rejected before I opened my mouth.

"Yes?" he said, tilting his head toward the young clerk as he watched me.

"This gentleman," said the young lady, with hardly any sarcasm, "is looking for antique jewelry—he says."

"Is that right? Pieces with a past, eh?"

"Right," I said.

For a second he stared at me with eyes so dark brown they looked black and then he smiled thinly, jerked his head and suggested we go back to his office. I followed him to a door which he opened, and I stepped past him, catching a whiff of shaving lotion. Then he moved past me and sat in a chair at a rolltop desk against the north wall. I took a chair to the right of the desk and glanced around the small, windowless room. It was about as gay as some of the cells I've slept in but smelled better. He certainly hadn't arranged it for receiving important customers.

"You're not a cop," he said.

"I know."

"Well, what are you?"

"Why can't I just be a jewelry customer?"

He shook his head. "You don't even wear a watch. You look like a bum."

"You're only off a couple days. Ever do any business with a guy named Bernie Cook?"

"Ah," he said, "so that's it."

"You knew him?"

"Some. He was a good customer for a while."

"Then he started getting his ice elsewhere, huh?"

"That's right. He found a wholesaler."

"You know who?"

"No. I gather it was a rather unconventional source."

"Stolen stuff?"

"That's what he wanted me to think."

"He offer you any bargains?"

"Oh, yes, but I don't think he was serious."

"Did he take any of your customers?"

He smiled tolerantly. "The jewelry business is not like bootlegging. We don't set up territories and have shoot-outs with the competition."

I said I could believe that but Bernie had done something to offend someone pretty thoroughly and I was just trying to figure out who it might have been.

"You should look for the parties that supplied him. Maybe they didn't do it voluntarily. An even better bet might be to talk with husbands of women he chased."

"Chased, or caught?"

"None of them were chaste, and most of them were caught. Women were Bernie's number one interest. Jewelry was just something he used for bait."

"You mean when he was your customer he wasn't always buying rocks for Trixie?"

"I knew him before he ever heard of her."

"Did he stop coming around when he married her?"

"No. He didn't stop completely until a year ago."

I thought things over for a moment while he watched me calmly. "You happen to know any of the women he was messing with recently?" I asked.

"He didn't tell. I didn't ask."

"I don't remember anybody ever had to ask Bernie to brag."

He smiled. "That's true. But we didn't meet recently and Bernie was always moving to something new. Besides, he lied a lot. I wouldn't want to slander anyone."

"You're about as loose-lipped as a Swiss banker," I said, getting to my feet.

"If I weren't, I wouldn't stay in this business long."

When I walked past the lady clerk she gave me a long, cool look and returned my grin and wave with a brief nod. Evidently she was at least some impressed by the fact her boss had given me so much time.

Chapter 11

That evening I went around to the Compton Hotel and found Rita in the dining room, having coffee after her dinner.

"Have you eaten?" she asked as I sat down.

"Yup," I admitted, looking enviously at the bare bone of her finished sirloin. From the redness of the remaining shreds I guessed she'd ordered it so rare it was breathing when they set it down.

She ordered coffee for me and apologized for not including brandy. "They don't serve liquor here."

"Fine." I didn't tell her I like brandy less than Scotch and I wouldn't feed Scotch to a warthog.

"What've you learned?" she asked.

"Nobody'll admit buying jewelry from Bernie."

"What's that mean?"

I explained about Howie's snooping and my follow-up on Trixie's report about jewelers.

Rita was so good to look at I didn't survey the place much until I'd finished two smokes and a couple cups of coffee and was looking around to

order another refill. That's when I spotted old Ike
Olson sitting at a small table near the tall windows
on the south side of the dining room. He had
company, a young, brown-haired girl with China doll
features, long fingers, and trim ankles. She was
dressed in black.

I looked too long and Rita asked if I knew the girl.

"No, but the guy's one of Bernie's poker players.
Ike Olson."

"The girl's young enough to be his daughter—
maybe his granddaughter."

"Uh-huh."

"I guess you'd like to go check them out."

I turned and found her frowning at me.

"Maybe I should. You mind?"

"Why should I mind?"

"I'll call you later."

"What for?"

"Well, I could give you a report and you could give
me the money you were going to have ready."

She tossed her head and said she hadn't forgotten
about that and didn't figure I would.

"Where'll you be?" I asked.

"Who knows? You can try the room. I don't know."

"I won't be long," I promised.

"Don't rush on my account."

Ike didn't seem overly delighted to see me at his
table, but he was old-timey enough to stand up.

"This is my daughter, Adair," he said.

She was wide-eyed, smooth skinned, glowing, and
clean. No rouge or powder, only red lipstick on a soft
mouth that at the moment drooped at the corners.
Her hazel eyes flicked over my face, first sad and
distant, then with sudden awareness when Ike gave
her my name.

"Who?"

Ike repeated it.

"I've heard of you," she said, frowning.

"Probably," said Ike. I couldn't tell what his tone was, it fell somewhere between disgust and resignation.

"Bernard played pool with you," she told me. "You beat him once."

I confessed to the accusation and kept secret the fact I'd beat him lots of times.

"I guess you knew him," I said.

She nodded mournfully and looked away.

I glanced at Ike who kept his eyes on his beautiful daughter.

"How well did you know Bernie?" I asked her.

"I loved him."

Ike winced and then, with an effort, glared at me.

"How long?" I asked.

"Forever," she said.

"She knew him three months," said Ike. "I introduced her, for Christ's sake."

She looked at me directly. "Did you like Bernard?"

"He was a good poker player."

"That's no answer."

"You're right," I admitted. "No, I can't say we were pals."

"What didn't you like?"

"He was such a liar. I don't mind that now and then, I do some lying myself, but it's hard to take a guy that *never* tells the truth."

"He couldn't help it."

Ike snorted.

"He couldn't," she insisted without looking at her father. "It was like somebody with a speech impediment, stuttering or lisping. It was just his way. It didn't mean he wasn't honest inside."

"Jesus," muttered Ike.

73

"He explained it to me," she went on, ignoring the old man. "It was something he did to make life more interesting. He said it kept his mind limber and his tongue free."

"It sure did," agreed Ike. "I never heard a freer tongue."

"It's better than being a drunkard or a mean person. He never told lies about people the way some folks do, to cause trouble and misery. They were mostly white lies or stories to make himself seem important. Bernard had a great need to be important, you know. That was his weakness. Nobody understood him."

"Only you and about a million other girls," said Ike, and then to me, "For Christ's sake, sit down, everybody's looking at us."

That was a slight exaggeration. Everybody at the moment consisted of two tables of people and I couldn't see that they were giving us any special attention, although they probably wondered what a guy like me was doing in such a spiffy place and how come I managed to talk with the two best-looking women who'd visited the dining room in the past twenty years.

I settled into a chair across from Ike and to Adair's left.

"Did Bernie tell you he beat me in poker?" I asked.

"Oh, yes. Was it true?"

"Pretty often."

"And you beat him more than once at pool, I bet."

I agreed and she laughed. She had a hell of a fine laugh, tilting her head back and letting me see her open mouth with unrepaired teeth all white and fine. She cut off abruptly, as if showing joy were a blasphemy against Bernard's recent loss.

"He said you were a very crazy guy. He told me things—"

"All lies," I assured her. "Did Bernie give you that ring?"

She lifted her left hand and gazed at the diamond on her engagement finger. It wasn't quite as big as a golf ball or small as a BB but if it was genuine I figured her future was secure as long as it wasn't stolen.

"Yes," she said. "He got it wholesale. It was only a loan."

"A loan?"

"Uh-huh. He loaned me lots of jewelry. I wore it when we met people he wanted to do business with. I modeled them, you could say."

Ike didn't groan out loud but his expression wouldn't have been too much different under questioning by the Spanish Inquisition.

"I guess I never heard of a model for jewelry before," I said.

"I don't suppose anybody ever thought of it before Bernard. He was a creative salesman. He said that fellows would see it on me and hope that by giving it to beautiful women, they'd win them over like he did me. Do you think he'd have wanted me to keep the jewels?"

"He probably thought you'd think so."

"Well, I didn't. I told him I couldn't accept such expensive things as presents."

"But on loan, it was okay?"

"Well, I was helping him."

"By just wearing the jewels and smiling pretty?"

She smiled pretty. "Don't you think that'd help him?"

Ike started to speak and she put her small hand on his arm and leaned toward him.

75

"Daddy, why don't you go on home? I'll talk some more with Mr. Wilcox and he'll bring me along when we're through, okay?"

Ike stared at her, closed his eyes, sighed, and stood up.

"Good night," he said, and left without looking at me.

Adair watched him go out and turned toward me. "How about him? Do you like him?"

"Yeah, he's all right."

"All right. I bet with you that means very okay. He's not a liar, huh?"

"Not by practice."

"You think I am?"

"Does it matter?"

"Yes," she said, and drew back, as if surprised.

"No, I don't think you're a liar. Maybe a little foolish. Was Bernie your lover?"

"A gentleman would never ask that question."

"A lady wouldn't be afraid to answer it."

"She wouldn't have to. *I* don't have to."

"Have you got any other jewelry Bernie loaned you?"

She nodded.

"What're you going to do with it?"

"I suppose you think I should give it to *her*?"

"Well, it was on loan, wasn't it?"

"Not from her."

"So now he's dead, it's all yours?"

She stared down at the table and wilted in a ladylike fashion. "I'd like to have *something*," she said in a tragic low tone. "The trouble is, nobody'd believe it was because I loved Bernard. They'd all think I was just a greedy girl. I wish he'd given me a *little* ring."

"Didn't he give you anything small?"

"Bernard didn't go for little things. He did give me one pair of small earrings, but I think they're pretty valuable."

"So what're you going to do?"

"I'll wait and see if they come to get them."

"Who's 'they'?"

"A couple of fellows Bernard knew."

"They got names?"

"There's one named Chuck, and the other he always called Mr. Stuckey."

I told her that sounded like a vaudeville team, but she insisted those were the names they used. Chuck was short and wide, Mr. Stuckey was tall and thin.

"Chuck's not really fat, you just think so at first glance. Bernard says—said—that he's terribly strong."

"He's got the jewels from them?"

"He never said, but that's what they talked about so I guessed they supplied them."

"What else did he tell you about them?"

"Nothing."

I didn't believe her and she knew it but didn't say any more. For a few seconds we sat there, not looking at each other. She stared off at the tables still occupied by two groups across the room. They were talking a lot and laughing often. A fat lady with short hair dyed black made her audience laugh every time she spoke and she seldom stopped talking.

"You don't approve of me, do you?" said Adair.

I met her eyes, so innocent and clear, and looked at her soft brown hair and the smoothly marcelled waves.

"I'm not strong on approving or disapproving."

"You disapprove, I can see it on your mouth."

"What's it like, green lipstick?"

"It's as plain."

I shook my head. "No, you're the one who's disapproving. You feel bad about upsetting your old man. You think you're awful to do that. None of us can please our old men. Any more than they can please us."

She leaned toward me. "So, you have troubles with your father too? Is he terribly old?"

"Older than Ike. I guess that's terrible to you."

"I suppose he doesn't like it that you don't dress fancy and have a steady job."

"That's right, he could forgive me drinking and maybe even going to jail if I looked smart and worked steady and didn't have so much fun."

"You've been in jail?" Her eyes popped until I was afraid they'd drop on the table and roll in my lap.

"Even prison. I guess Bernie didn't tell you all about me after all."

She blushed a little and her eyes settled back. "Maybe he told me and I didn't take it seriously. After all, I hadn't met you yet and he talked about lots of people he knew."

"But not about Mr. Stuckey and Chuck?"

She put her elbows on the table and crossed her wrists while looking around the dining room. The fat lady and her gang had left, the other group was getting to its feet. Adair looked at me sideways.

"I think he was afraid to talk about them. He never kidded when they were around."

"So you met them?"

"Oh, yes. At that speakeasy where Bernard always went. They came in and sat down with us. They didn't wait to be invited. Mr. Stuckey just smiled nice, but the other one, Chuck, he looked at Bernard like he was mad at him. Mr. Stuckey had real hollow cheeks, wispy hair and long arms and big, bony hands. He was real polite to me and hardly drank at all, just held a beer bottle in his big hands. I tried to keep my eyes on him because after the squat one quit glaring at Bernard he started watching me with his little bitty, mean eyes. His hands are thick and his fingers look like sausages. God, I hate hands like that, don't you?"

"Yeah. What'd they talk about?"

"I couldn't follow it at all. Mr. Stuckey said something about interest on an investment and while he kept smiling nice all the time, I could tell Bernard was scared. He bought their drinks and talked real loud and fast. After they'd gone he didn't talk at all. I asked if they'd threatened him and he laughed and said of course not, he was too valuable to them. They'd never hurt him, only maybe kill him a little. He wanted me to think that was a joke, but it wasn't."

"When'd this happen?"

"In May, a little after he loaned me the jewelry."

"Did you see these guys again?"

She shook her smooth head and folded her hands. "Let's not talk about them anymore. Where have you been in jail?"

"It'd almost be easier to say where not."

"What'd you do?"

"The main crime was being broke. That's very serious. Drunk had something to do with it now and then, but that's only serious if you don't have any money."

She stared at me with such fascination I wondered if I might manage to be Bernie's successor.

"Have you been in prison?" she asked.

I admitted I had. She asked what for.

"Cattle rustling and trying to rob a jewelry store."

"Did you always try to rob rich people?"

"Hell, yes. What's the percentage in robbing the poor?"

"That's what Bernard said. I never felt bad that maybe the jewelry he had was stolen. People that own things like that have more than they need or deserve."

"You've thought about that a lot, huh?"

"Now you're making fun of me."

"Not a bit. Do you know where I could find these ice men?"

"You mean Chuck and Mr. Stuckey?"

"Right."

"No. But I guess they know where to find me."

She wasn't comforted by that notion and her bright face turned gloomy.

"Does Ike know these guys?"

She shook her head. "I hope they don't come around when he's home. He might do something foolish."

"There shouldn't be any trouble if you just turn over the jewels."

"You'd ought to know Dad better than that. If they came in, threatening at all, he'll get excited and maybe do something foolish."

"Has he got a gun?"

"Sure. And sometimes, when he goes gambling, he has a knife strapped to his ankle."

No wonder the old bastard had always been so gutsy in spite of his years. Loaded with equalizers, hip and ankle.

"If you had the chance," I said, "would you let me know when these guys come around?"

She looked at me with her innocent eyes. "I know a better way."

"How's that?"

"I'll just give the jewelry to you. When they come

around I'll tell them you've got it all for safe keeping."

I stared at her, marveling at the deviousness of youth. "Why not turn the stuff over to the cops?"

"I think that'd make those fellows mad."

"You think they'll be tickled pink that you turned it over to me?"

"They won't be as mad as if it were the cops," she answered.

"Uh-huh. And if these two guys never show, the jewels won't be a total loss, huh?"

"I hadn't thought of that."

"I'll bet. And if the cops happen around your way, you'll claim Bernie never gave you anything but a good time."

She nodded serenely.

"How come, knowing my record, you trust me?" I asked.

"I think Bernard did. And I don't have much other choice, do I?"

"Okay," I agreed, "let's go see this loot."

Ike was in the parlor listening to a radio show when we came in and he gave me a fishy eye.

"Jesus," he said. "You'd think a man like me could raise a kid with some sense in picking guys."

She told him not to be stupid and me to wait while she went upstairs for the stuff.

Ike, still in a grouch, got up, snapped the radio off and sat down again. He about disappeared in the high-backed easy chair and propped his small feet on the footstool.

"What's she after?" he demanded.

"Stuff Bernie left her."

"I'll bet it's phony."

"You know what it is?"

He turned to a smoking stand beside his chair, opened the door, got a cigar from a box inside, hesitated a second, then asked if I wanted one. I shook my head. He unwrapped a cigar, lit it, let out smoke, and tilted his head back.

"Jewelry," he said.

"How long ago did he give it to her?"

"I didn't see any till the last month or so."

"You said she'd only known Bernie three months. She told me she'd known him for a year."

His eyes glittered angrily. "Who knows who his kids know and what the hell they do? And what the hell difference does it make?"

"I like to know who's lying to who, that's one difference. And the longer people know each other, the more involved things get. She was involved good, it looks like."

"Good, hell."

He retreated behind a cloud of smoke and about then Adair showed up. She put a small cigar box on an end table beside my chair and sat down nearby. I opened the box. A piece of blue velvet covered the bottom and over it she'd spread four rings, a couple of earrings, a brooch, two stickpins and a few necklaces. They sparkled under the lamplight. Adair watched me, waiting for a gasp or maybe a greedy grin, but since I don't know diamonds from glass and there was no way to guess what it might be worth, I just gawked. Ike held still for about one or two seconds, then had to get up and bring over his cloud of cigar smoke.

"Huh!" he grunted. "That's not exactly a pirate's treasure. He give that all to you at once?"

"No. Mostly one now and another later."

"What the hell'd he get in exchange?"

"He didn't have to buy me," she told him in a tight voice. "Not everybody's for sale."

He was awfully quick for an old man. His backhand caught her flush on the cheek and snapped her head hard enough to make her marcelled hair flip.

"Hey!" I said, moving between them. "Hold on—"

Adair came to her feet, eyes blazing, claws up and lips back in a snarl. Ike tried to throw off my hand, but I had his thin wrist tight and he suddenly gave it up. I was damned relieved when Adair pulled back at the same time.

The way they both backed into their corners made me worry; I can weather screaming, pitched crockery and stomping around, but when family folk are too mad to even yell, it spooks me.

I stuck around, hoping it would give them time to cool off and talked some about how I'd have the stuff appraised to see if it was really valuable enough for hoods to be interested. After a few minutes of monologue I got up again and picked up the cigar box from the little table. Ike shuffled off without a glance at either of us.

"Is everything in here?" I asked Adair.

"Yeah," she said, without meeting my eyes.

"You hang on to something and these guys really show up, you could get me in big trouble."

"It's all there," she insisted angrily. She was so mad I knew she was lying.

"Except the ring on your finger."

"I'll give that to them myself."

"You do that."

Chapter 12

It was nearly ten when I left Olson's carrying that trouble magnet under my arm. A smart guy, I figured, would dump it on Lieutenant Baker, only that'd just give him another reason to believe Trixie had done in her wayward hubby and make the hoods vindictive toward Adair, not to mention me.

I shoved the box under the seat of the Model T, cranked up the engine and headed downtown. It was too late to drop in on Rita unannounced so I found a telephone and called.

"Things got complicated," I said when she answered with a grumpy "Yes?"

"I can imagine," she said.

"Don't imagine too much. Can I see you now?"

"I hope not."

"You're ready for bed?"

"I'm ready for sleep."

My imagination worked on that. "How do you sleep?" I asked.

"Very well."

"That wasn't what I meant."

"I know it. So eat your heart out—you just ruined tonight."

"I'm trying to work on a job for your sister. You want me to dog that?"

"I suppose you made a lot of progress?"

"Some, yeah. I've got another lead, maybe two. And I kept a father and daughter from having a cat fight."

"What started it, you?"

"If we get together I can tell you about it."

She was silent for a moment, I suppose trying to decide whether she was more curious than annoyed or sleepy.

"You don't strike me as an early-to-bed girl."

"I'm not an early-to-sleep girl, you can count on that."

"So get unready for sleep and we'll talk."

"All right, pick me up out front. Don't come in, I'll be out when I see your car."

A few minutes later I pulled up and she popped out of the hotel and in beside me.

"What do you do," I asked, "sleep in your dress?"

"I don't sleep in anything, and it doesn't take long to get into this. Let's go."

She didn't want to drink or eat, she wanted to know what I'd learned, so I drove along nice and easy and told her about the Olsons. Everything but that Adair had turned over the jewelry to me. I'm not sure why I held that back; I guess it's because I always need to save some secrets from women I don't really know. Maybe even ones I know best.

"Do you think the police know Bernie was messing with Adair?" asked Rita.

I said I doubted it. As long as they had Trixie in

such a tight package they weren't likely to knock themselves out checking all the angles.

"Aren't you going to tell them about her?"

"Yeah, sooner or later. There'd ought to be somebody keeping an eye on her."

"You sure you don't want to handle that job yourself?"

"No, it might be more than I can handle," I told her.

"The job or the girl?"

"Either or both. Are you really trying to make me think you're jealous of that kid?"

"Don't flatter yourself, buster. I just want you to mind the business you're in."

"That's just what the hell I'm doing. Anybody involved with Bernie is part of the business and following up on them is the only way I know to save your sister's neck."

"Okay, why don't you park this thing so you don't have to watch the road all the time?"

That seemed like a great notion. I headed for the park on the north side and pulled up beside a little dam on Quenton Creek. The moon was just a sliver in the southwest and the sparkly sky reflected in the black water before us.

Rita stared through the windshield for a few seconds before turning to me. "You really think you can help Trixie?"

When I turned to face her she looked out again, letting me take in her profile. She held it steady so I could get the picture clear and it was damned nice.

I sighed and decided to be honest. "No. I don't think there's a chance."

She faced me again. "But you'll try?"

"Sure."

"You won't just go through the motions—"

"I never just go through motions."

"That's what I figured," she said, and put her left hand on my shoulder. "Trixie's crazy, I know it, so do you, but she's sweet and good and we've got to help her. I'll make it worth your while—any way and every way. You understand that?"

"Don't get too carried away, you might distract me."

"I don't think I could. I haven't so far."

"You haven't made a real try."

Her fingers kneaded my shoulder lightly.

"You're a strong and dangerous man. I didn't just see that in your palm. I know men pretty well, and I'm not just bragging, believe me."

I grinned at her. "You don't have to vamp me into anything, honey."

"Wouldn't you like me to?"

I wanted her to in the worst way, and at the same time I didn't much like the notion of being seduced as an incentive to services rendered—or being used. I like a lay anywhere I can get it, but it's usually better when I think it comes because I'm irresistible and not for something I can do outside of bed.

"You're a very different kind of guy," she said. "I've never known anyone like you before . . ."

I'd heard it before, loved it, swallowed it whole. Any guy who's heard it has thought, oh, yeah, you're so right, how come nobody ever saw it before? Tell me more, lots more . . .

She asked me to tell about myself and of course I did. I passed over the bumming pretty quick, I figured the cowboying and sign painting, poker games and close calls would sell, but she wanted mostly to know how a man could live on nothing and seem to like it.

"Does it make you feel more free—is that what's so

important to you? Not owning or owing—no responsibilities?"

"Mostly it's what's going to be down the track, in the next town or state, hobo jungle or boxcar. The thing of being on the move is all a matter of momentum. You start to roll and you don't want to stop, nothing counts but the horizon."

"When do you stop?"

"When you find out there's no place to go."

"You mean, when you've been everywhere?"

"You've never been everywhere. Nobody ever lived long enough. But you find out there's nothing that different. Some's better, some's worse, but all the people are strangers and you're no-account."

"So you come back home."

"That's right, like the fella said, that's where they got to take you in."

"What's it like, where you live?"

"The town?"

"No, the place where you sleep."

"It's a room in the Wilcox Hotel, about eight by ten feet with one window, a half bed, a bureau and a straight-backed chair. I got a great view of the privet hedge, a box elder and Doverman's Garage just across the graveled driveway out back of the hotel. There's a footlocker at the bottom of the bed."

"Are you satisfied with that?"

"On rainy nights in summer and any night in winter, it beats a blanket on the ground."

"But you've slept on the ground lots of times?"

"Oh, yeah."

"I've never done that."

"Try it. It'll make you appreciate a bed like nothing else can."

She shook her head. "I don't have to cut myself to know it's nice not to bleed."

I grinned and told her she was wise beyond her years. How about the place where she slept, what was it like?"

"It's fluffy and white and roomy. The bed is full size and has a canopy and there are two big windows with filmy curtains and heavy drapes. There's a chaise longue and a big dresser with three-way mirrors and spindly legs, and my carpet is deep and a million colors. There's a little bathroom all pink and a white tub with claw feet—"

"And sometimes you have breakfast in bed at noon?"

"Sometimes."

"What do you do to earn all that?"

"Who says I earn it?"

"Well, it's not likely you inherited a fortune since Sister Trixie isn't rich, so you must have some system."

"My own daddy didn't provide, so I got a new daddy who does."

"Ah."

"Don't 'Ah!' so damned wise. I'm as free as you are."

"Uh-huh. As long as daddy lasts. Then what?"

"I'll find another."

I studied her and finally nodded.

"What else have you done?" she asked.

"Spent a year beachcombing in the Philippines."

"How was it?"

"Beat panhandling in the States."

"Why'd you quit?"

"Got lonesome for snow. All those days with nothing but sun, one day like the last, no seasons. Gets monotonous as heaven."

She grinned. "You figure you'll get more variety in hell?"

"I've decided to skip them both."

"Well, we've got something else in common."

We kept talking and I wanted to start something, but she didn't give me another lead so I waited, trying to figure out what she really wanted. What spoiled it mostly was that there'd been this talk of paying me for help, and I didn't feel like asking her to fork it over at the same time I was trying to get under her clothes.

Principles are generally a pain in the ass.

Finally I drove her back to the hotel and before she got out of the car she dug in her purse and handed over an envelope. I said thanks and felt foolish.

"This is fun," she said, leaning down to look at me from the curb. "Now I feel like a sugar mama."

Chapter 13

So I was all fixed up with advance money, about a dozen suspects and not the foggiest notion of what to do next. After a night's sleep and breakfast at the Wilcox Hotel, I went over to see Boswell. He was resting on his bunk when I came in and lay there, blinking up at me while I gave his cluttered place the once over. Patsy, who'd been dozing by his feet, lifted her thin head, opened her mouth in a dog grin and waggled her stump tail.

"Resting from your exertions?" I asked.

Boswell sat up slowly, pushed his tousled hair back and yawned.

"I was thinking," he said.

"What about?"

"Whether I'd still make moon when liquor comes back."

"You will if it doesn't come back free, and it won't."

"I ain't sure."

"You think it'll be free?"

"No, I ain't sure I'll keep making it. It's a lot of bother and it ain't really good. Besides, when it's legal, it'll be cheaper."

"By golly," I said, "you really have been bending your skull on the question."

After a while he asked how I was coming on my mystery.

"If it was going good, I wouldn't be here, and you know it."

He nodded and when Patsy moved against his shin he reached down to pull her ears gently.

"I've found out old Barnyard was peddling hot jewelry around Aquatown. Even hung some of it on his girl friend and paraded her around to promote it. Can you beat that?"

"He was a show-offy fella."

"He was a damned fool. But everybody involved must have been. This girl's story makes it sound like a couple big city hoods had turned the stuff over to Barnyard to sell for them and they'd been around to let him know they wanted money. It could be they figured he'd just given it to the girl so they stuck a pillow over his head after Trixie'd left the body neatly tied to the bed. That kind of thing appeals to guys like that."

Boswell thought that over for about a week and then shook his head.

"What's the matter?" I asked.

"Well, wouldn't it seem kind of lucky if these two bad fellas just happened around when Trixie and Bernard were doing what they did?"

"Hell, these guys probably knew his routine. He played poker every Friday night and everybody knew what happened after. Barnyard blabbed it all over."

"But she didn't always go off and leave him tied up, did she?"

I squinted at him. "You're pretty smart for such an old fart."

He gave me his innocent look.

"It could also be," I said, "that Trixie found out about Barnyard's messing with this young girl, giving her diamonds to wear and all, and tipped off the crooks when she'd set Barnyard up."

"But she'd have known it'd look like she done it."

"Not if he'd been blasted, gangland style. Maybe they double-crossed her. That'd help explain why she's holding out on me."

Boswell shook his head sorrowfully. It was all too much for him and he put it aside while he bent down and scratched Patsy's head between her ears. She stood up to make it easy.

"I wish to hell I could be sure Trixie didn't do it or manage it."

Boswell peered at me through his bushy eyebrows.

"The trouble is," I said, "a woman like Trixie, sometimes she goes a little screwy because nobody ever takes her seriously. She spends her life being a combination doxy, decoration, and amusement parlor. When she gets mad, guys laugh and tell her she's a spitfire and slap her on the ass. They even stay tolerant when she gets a little rough. A girl like that, she can reach a time when she wants somebody to know she means business."

Boswell nodded.

"She could have got carried away when she had him all trussed up like a Thanksgiving turkey," I went on. "She could've pounded him till he was so mad she was afraid to let him free. He wasn't the killing kind but get him mad enough, he might've hit

93

her in the face and she could stand anything but somebody messing up her looks."

"Mebbe." He was unconvinced.

"The trouble is, about a million other people'd like to have killed the bastard."

Boswell sighed in sympathy and got up.

"Say something," I told him.

"You want some moon?"

"Yeah, but I can't. I'm working."

Boswell is the only man I know who wouldn't be stunned by that response; he simply nodded and looked sympathetic. Since sympathy doesn't inspire me, I decided to go back to the hotel.

Elihu glared at me from his swivel chair by the window next to the front door. I stopped beside him, rolled a cigarette, lit it, and smiled.

"You plan to be using that room upstairs anymore?" he demanded.

"Why? You got somebody wants it?"

"I might. We rent out rooms here, you know. That's the business we're in."

"Oh? I thought you just raised bedbugs."

"You're funnier than a broken crutch. One of these days you're gonna come around here and find your junk sitting out on the walk."

"Well, what do you think you'd ought to get paid for that cubbyhole?"

"Seventy-five cents a night, five dollars a week. You rented rooms enough to know that."

"That's for rooms big enough to hold a full bed. Mine's worth fifty cents a night, three and a quarter a week. And that includes showers."

"Once a week," he said.

"Not when I take 'em cold."

He snorted but accepted the three and a quarter, got up, carried it to the register and rang it up. He was dying to ask where I got the money but couldn't bring himself to offer me an opening for some wise-ass answer. Mostly he preferred not to know because he figured it hadn't come honestly—that is, screwed out of somebody that needed something I had to sell.

I'd finished my cold shower and had just put on fresh duds when there was a knock at my door. I opened it and there was Ma, drawn up to her full five feet, arms folded, mouth set.

"Where'd you get money?" she demanded.

"You'll be happier not knowing."

"Being happy where you're concerned is something I forgot about too long ago to remember. Have you got a job?"

"I have."

"Doing what?"

I thought of saying I was hired to please a lady but remembered she'd had heart problems and decided it was too risky.

"I'm doing a little investigation in Aquatown."

She pursed her lips. "Another murder?"

"I'm afraid so."

"Well, I guess that's better than gambling."

"I don't know. The hours aren't much different and the company's about as bad."

"You get paid whether you find the man or not?"

"Either way. Even got an advance."

"Don't drink it up."

I grinned at her and she frowned back.

"Was it that gambler that got killed, is that the case?"

I admitted it was.

"So the man that did it won't want you finding out about him, eh?"

"That figures."

She nodded. "Be careful," she said, and hurried off.

Her rare concern touched me until I remembered that I'd suddenly become a paying guest and that was the real reason she hoped I wouldn't get killed.

When I drifted around to see Trixie late in the afternoon both Rita and Howie were in attendance. Rita wore a white dress with a high collar that set off her black hair so she looked like something from a movie ad. I didn't notice what Howie wore. Trixie was raging because she'd convinced herself she'd get bail and they'd let her out, but Howie couldn't swing it. There was no talking to her under the circumstances and eventually the three of us not behind bars yet went down to the Cozy Café and huddled in a booth.

Howie said that if I could come up with the least little thing he might be able to get Trixie out until the trial.

"She's probably better off where she is," I said.

"What do you mean?" demanded Rita.

"The guys Bernie got the hot goods from may be the ones that handled the pillow. If they did and she got out, they might figure she could blow the whistle and that'd make them try for insurance."

"But that'd spoil the frame," said Howie.

"If the judge let her out, they'd figure the frame didn't fit and they'd play it straight and ice her."

"Why'd *they* want to kill Bernard?" asked Rita.

"Lots of reasons. He turned over a mess of their rocks to a new girl friend. He might have wanted out and they didn't trust him. Hell, he lied all the time, all it'd take is one big slip and they'd wipe him out. Those guys don't take chances."

"Yeah," said Howie, cheering up. "I'll explain that to Trixie. It might help her to adjust.

When he was gone Rita looked me over with a cold eye and asked, "What've you done since you got paid?"

"Showered, shaved, changed clothes, paid a week's advance on my room and got a night's sleep. What's the matter, isn't it any fun being a sugar mama after the first glow?"

We drank coffee and didn't look at each other for a while. I guessed she hadn't slept much the night before. Most people who can't sleep turn owly because nobody ever lays awake thinking of good things for long. Everything but making love is lousy in the dark; there's no promise in it. I don't see how blind people can stay human.

"What're you going to do next?" Rita asked.

"Talk to everybody again. Bounce some of the stuff I've learned off them. Maybe push enough to make one or two of them defensive. Meanwhile something else might pop. A couple city boys Bernie was messing with may come around soon to take care of unfinished business."

She wanted to hear more about that, but I said let's wait until I see if there's anything to it.

"All right," she said, gathering up her purse and gloves. "Call me tonight. I want to know what's going on. I've got that much coming."

"Is that it? Or do you just want to be sure I'm staying sober?"

She looked me dead in the eye. "There's that."

"What time shall I call?"

"Midnight."

"I'm supposed to be working till then?"

"Why not? You haven't done anything yet today, have you?"

She didn't smile when I grinned and admitted I hadn't, and while I was paying the cashier for our coffee she left the café and was half a block down the street by the time I stepped into the bright sunlight and blinked after her. Even a half a block away you could see what a fine figure of a woman she was. Some day, I told myself, I had to persuade her that Carl was okay. It shouldn't be too hard; I'd just have to learn who smothered her brother-in-law, spring her sister, and not make it look too easy. Not making it look easy should be a cinch.

Chapter 14

Johanson's wife answered the phone when I called his house and I asked her what time he usually got home.

"God knows."

"You mean some nights he never makes it?"

"He always makes it, I just never know when. Cement crews can't just quit when they think it's time."

"Does he sometimes stop on the way for a drink?"

"Now what in the world would make a man like you think of a thing like that?"

"Being a man, I guess. You know where he stops?"

"No, I don't know anything about speakeasys and I don't want to. Why don't you just drop by later in the evening? I'll give you coffee and a piece of pie if you like."

I told her that was the best offer I'd had all month, and she asked what more did I expect to learn from Joe. I admitted I had no idea.

"Well," she said, "you'll find out it was Bernie's wife that killed him."

"You're sure of that, eh?"

"Positive. She's evil. You can tell, just looking at her, if you're not a man. She fools all of you."

"You think she had her hooks out for Joe?"

"Anything in pants."

I began to wonder if I should check up on Joe Johanson's movements Friday night but said nothing about that and after a few seconds more chatter, rang off.

When I drifted into Schuman's Clothing Store I was greeted by a pressed and shined, clean-shaven and hard-brushed older man standing guard near the front counter. He took in my shapeless pants, scuffed shoes, and rumpled shirt and decided I was going to ask for a handout.

"Hi," I said. "Is Gene Healey around?"

My familiarity bred contempt, but I looked disreputable enough to keep him fairly cautious.

"He's busy out back," he said, almost politely. "Can I help you?"

"Yeah, you could ask him to come up front."

I stared at him hard and smiled soft. He looked apprehensive but hung tough.

"Are you a regular customer of his?"

"Sure, doesn't it show?"

"Well . . ." he began as Gene came out of the back room carrying a box of shirts. His face didn't exactly light up when he spotted me, but after a second's pause he came forward.

"This gentleman wants to see you," said the dated fashion model, and huffed off.

"That the boss?" I asked, tilting my head.

"Uh—yeah. What do you want?"

"How you fixed for tuxedos?"

"You're kidding."

"You're right."

He grinned and I grinned back and said I was after information.

"We don't sell that. You buy a suit or a pair of pants, I can talk."

"How about I buy a pair of sox?"

"Naw, you'd buy a dime pair and that's not worth the time you've already taken. How about after work? I'll meet you at Fino's."

Fino's was a mansion a banker built about 1900. Back then it was just two blocks off the mainstem and now it was surrounded by commercial buildings that left it looking like a dowager duchess at a Rotary meeting. Most speakeasys have a side or back entrance. Fino's opened in front where the only black man in South Dakota met customers, took their hats and whatever, and ushered them inside where they found a grand staircase that led to about half a million rooms. Most of these had from three to four tables; some, I'm told, had only one with a couch for private parties. And of course there were big banquet rooms. The after-work crowd mostly gathered in the big dining room at the L-shaped bar or the dinky tables scattered around. Heavy drapes covered the bay windows and gaslights along the walls gave the place a shadowy warmth.

Right off I spotted Johanson at the bar. I ambled over, hoisted a cheek onto the stool to his right and waved for a beer. Joe turned his hawk beak my way and scowled.

"Who told you I was here?"

"Nobody. I'm meeting Gene Healey."

He didn't believe me and I wondered why he'd think I was making a point of finding him.

"We finished early," he told me. "That's the last job we got lined up for this month."

"So you stopped to celebrate?"

"Some guys don't celebrate being out of work. Some guys got to support a family."

"Don't growl at me, Joe. I'm not living on any inheritance, you know."

He sipped from his shot glass, chased it with a little water from the tumbler by his right hand and stared glumly at the mirror behind the bar.

"Where do you figure you'll be playing poker from now on?" I asked.

"Probably won't have enough money to play anywhere."

I turned on the stool after paying for my beer and looked the room over. There were lots of guys around but few I recognized and none I really knew. Just as I was turning back toward Joe, Gene Healey came through the door, waved, and joined us.

"Let's get a table," he said.

Joe wasn't thrilled by the notion but obviously was in no hurry to get home so we all sat down together in a corner and Gene made small talk until he got his beer.

"Where do you figure you'll be playing poker now?" I asked.

"Probably at Ike's," said Gene.

"You figure his daughter can take Trixie's place?"

"Jesus, don't ever talk like that around Ike—he'll slice up your gizzard."

"You know his daughter?"

"Sure," Gene said. ·

Joe got a wise look. "Bernie knew her too."

Gene frowned his disapproval and glanced at me.

"That sounds," I said to Joe, "as if you thought he knew her real well."

"He did," said Joe, ignoring Gene.

"You don't know that for a fact," said Gene.

"I don't know for a fact that Bernie's dead either—but I believe it."

"Did Ike know Bernie was messing with his daughter?" I asked.

Joe shrugged. I looked at Gene. He looked away.

"Come on," I said. "Are you two guys trying to tell me Ike had a good reason to kill Bernie, or are you trying to keep me from the notion? Make up your minds."

"Ike wouldn't have smothered him," said Gene. "He might've shot him or even knifed him, but he wouldn't stick a pillow over him when he was tied down."

"But you think he knew what was going on, don't you?"

They both nodded.

"How could you be sure?"

"Ike's attitude that Friday night," said Gene. "Other times, when Bernie used Trixie to get some mug all fouled up, Ike didn't pay any attention, but that Friday, whooee! He burned. Kept saying Bernie should stop fucking around and goddamn play poker. He never talked like that with Trixie hanging around and he hated to let Bernie see he was sore."

"How come nobody ever mentioned this before?"

"Well, I hadn't thought too much about the evening before," Gene said, "and I didn't want to say anything that'd make anybody figure I was fingering anybody, you know?"

"I noticed you didn't have any trouble about fingering Trixie," I said.

"Well, hell, Carl, it was all so obvious. I didn't think I was *accusing* her."

"No, you just flat out said she did it."

"Well, golly, she had plenty reasons."

"So did Ike, from what you guys say. So why'd you want to protect him?"

"He's one of us," said Joe.

I looked to see if he was kidding and met his straight, sober gaze. It said Trixie was a woman and that was supposed to explain everything.

I took a swig of beer, built a cigarette, lit it, and leaned back.

"It's funny," I said. "I don't remember Trixie ever wearing a kimono when I was around. Usually wore a housedress. Once in a while a party outfit with a low front. How come all of a sudden she's in a floozie outfit?"

They looked at each other and Joe shrugged.

"You never noticed?" I asked Joe.

"Hell, I never paid any attention to what she wore. I went there to play cards."

Gene grinned at him. "Sure."

Joe glowered. "You calling me a liar?"

Gene was all innocence. "Never."

"Do either one of you guys know if she ever put out to any of the players?" I asked.

"She never put out for *me*," said Gene, who'd evidently decided it was dangerous to pretend he'd been cozy.

"Me either," said Joe. He didn't sound so much certain as sad.

"How about the others?"

"I don't know about you," said Gene.

"What about Ike?"

"Too old," said Gene. "He couldn't get it up."

"Don't bet on that," said Joe.

"You think he did?" I asked him.

"Didn't say that. Just said don't bet he couldn't."

"Did anybody you remember besides this Podolack get to see Trixie's colors while you were around?"

Gene thought that over seriously while Joe gazed around the speakeasy. Then Joe chugalugged his beer and stood up.

"Gotta go home," he said. "See you."

We watched him weave his way between tables and disappear through the distant door.

"He was hot for Trixie, wasn't he?" I said.

"Weren't we all?"

"Yeah, but he was serious about it."

He shrugged.

"What'd you do that night after you left Bernie's?"

He laughed. "What do you think? I came over here."

"I thought you blew your roll in the game."

"Just my betting money. I never blow my drinking money."

We talked some more without my getting any new line and when we parted he shook my hand. It was as if he didn't expect to see me again.

I blew a nickel calling Rita who agreed to meet with me and a few minutes later I was in the hotel. She looked fine coming down the steps in her black dress and black shoes. Her hips swayed smoothly and her eyes were steady on mine until she halted a yard away and looked me over.

"You aren't exactly Beau Brummel," she said. "What kind of a joint are you taking me to?"

"One that'll let me in, even if I bring a lady above my class."

"Uh-huh. They probably figure that way they'll get paid."

"Nobody skips the bill in a speakeasy."

"So you've still got some of my money left."

"Yeah, but this meal is business. It goes on the expense account."

"Maybe I'd better go change into my business clothes."

"What you're wearing means business to me. Let's go."

Rita liked Fino's. The lights were low, there were all kinds of guys and every one of them gave her the eye as we were led through the bar to one of the smaller rooms on the north side. It wasn't private—there were two other tables, still unoccupied—but it was, as she said, intimate, and she looked around approvingly at the white table cloth, silverplate utensils, and sparkling glasses. An ogling waiter took our drink orders and left.

"Not bad," she said. "Not bad at all. Where's the menu?"

"You can have anything you like as long as it's chicken or ribs, both barbecued. They're good."

She grinned at me. Her eyes half closed and her even teeth gleamed in the dim light. I'm never surprised when women are moody, almost every one I've known except my sister was that way, switching from hot to cold, sweet to sour, cozy to distant, and some of them went through the whole business all in half an hour. It could be a pain, but it often made things damned interesting. By and large guys are more comfortable to be around, but women are a hell of a lot more fun. I don't suppose it's just the moods that make the difference. . . .

"Well, mister, what's the business of this meeting?"

"I need your help to make Trixie level with me.

Something screwy was going on during Bernie's last night and I've got to find out what it was."

"After all the stuff she's already admitted, what do you think she'd hold back?"

"Something about why she was only wearing a kimono that night, why there was so much more tease going on with this Podolack guy than there'd ever been with the rest of us. As far as anybody knows, this guy just happened along—didn't have any dough or connections. So what was the big deal?"

"Okay, I'll try to find out."

Her mood changed again when the waiter came back and we both ordered ribs. She ate quickly and started asking questions before I was half way through my meal. I told her a couple of the ways I'd got my nose broken and described some of the lighter sides of being a hobo. I skipped the cold, hunger, lice, and really bad parts about hobo jungles. I even told her what it was like beachcombing in the Philippines.

"Was it living in all that sun that made you so dark?"

"Naw, I was born this way."

I tried to make her talk about herself, but she evaded me with a smoothness that showed lots of practice and I didn't press.

The two guys appeared out of the shadows of the alley as we reached my car. One was tall, the other short, and I guessed they were Mr. Stuckey and Chuck, the ice men.

"We'll take our car," Mr. Stuckey told me. He stood close with his hands dangling at his sides.

Chuck's hands were in his pockets. He didn't look fat or cheerful; he was more like wide and mean.

"Why?" I asked.

"Who?" demanded Rita.

"A young lady left some stuff of ours with you," said the tall man. "We want it."

"It's not that simple," I said.

"Oh?" Mr. Stuckey sounded almost polite. His sidekick muttered something not polite at all.

"The stuff's in Corden. You give me your address and I'll deliver it tomorrow."

"Uh-huh, tomorrow never comes. Our car's behind yours, get in it."

"Okay," I said, and then, turning to Rita, "Why don't you just run along?"

"No," said Chuck. "She comes along."

He reached for her and she jerked back, gripped my left arm, and hurried us toward their car. They followed almost in lock step. When we stopped, Chuck moved around, opened the front door and waved for me to get in. I shook my head and said I'd ride with the lady. Stuckey's hand dipped toward his right pocket. Rita said "Now!" and whipped her large purse in a sharp arc that ended abruptly between Chuck's legs. I hooked Stuckey with a left to the gut and spun to my right as Rita brought her purse down on Chuck's lowered skull. He gasped, staggered, and lifted his head just in time to catch my knee in his kisser. His gun rattled on the street before he collapsed, and as they both relaxed I grabbed Rita and took off for my tin lizzie.

We were half a block away before she turned to ask who were they and what was it all about.

"Hoods from the cities. They supplied Bernie with hot jewelry he was supposed to peddle around here."

"Where do you come in?"

I told her about my deal with Adair.

"So why didn't you just turn the stuff over to them?"

"I don't think Adair gave me all she had. And these guys aren't the types you can explain a lot to in a nice friendly way."

"You sure won't now."

"No. What made you swing on Chuck?"

"Didn't you see him eyeing me? Like a starved hog watching the trough get filled. *Nothing* would've made me get in back with that animal."

"You could've been killed."

"With guys like that, anything can get you killed. I wasn't ready to leave the choice up to them. Besides, I've heard enough about you to know you'd move."

"What the hell do you carry in that bag?"

"Lots, but five rolls of quarters do the job."

"Wouldn't a blackjack be handier?"

"No, sir. You can't carry one of those around in your hand and comes an emergency, you can't spend it."

We pulled up in front of her hotel and I turned off the engine, leaned back and gazed at her.

"I thought I'd been around, but I never, in my life, came across your equal. Not even close."

She smiled. "You're pretty good yourself."

"Would you let me hold that bag for a minute?"

"Why?"

"I don't want it in your hands when I kiss you."

She slipped it from her lap and leaned my way.

It didn't surprise me that kissing her wasn't like pecking a maiden aunt, but I hadn't expected it to hit me like a quart of moon. When she drew away I didn't have strength enough to hang on; I just

109

sat there with my mouth open and my eyes glazed. A slight movement outside brought me to, and I spotted an old geezer standing on the walk, staring at us with his jaw sagging.

Rita opened her door and began edging out. "Call me tomorrow," she said.

I reached for her arm, but she slipped clear and stepped to the sidewalk.

"Don't call too early."

"How about five?"

"If it's P.M."

"Why don't you get back in here? We'll go somewhere—"

"Uh-uh. Those two fellows might show up. Don't worry, we'll get together good when things level off, okay?"

"How level does it have to get?"

"Call me tomorrow."

"I'm not likely to forget."

The old guy moved aside to let her pass and stood staring with me as she went up the steps to the hotel. Then he looked back my way, blinking.

"That's all the show for tonight, pal," I said. "Sorry."

He sighed and slowly shuffled off.

Chapter 15

I wasn't sleepy, didn't like the notion of driving back to Corden for my paid bed, and decided the only thing to do was head back to Fino's.

The place was mobbed and I didn't see Tiny until I'd bellied up to the bar and ordered a beer. He was way across the room at a table with a small blonde. After paying for my suds I drifted his way. I wasn't sure whether he'd seen me but saw him lean toward the lady, who got up without looking around and left.

"I hope that wasn't my fault," I said when I halted beside the abandoned chair.

Tiny looked up with his monstrous baby face and beamed as though I were his long-lost mother. "Carl! Sit down, how are you?"

"As my old uncle used to say, 'Worse.' I guess auctioneers don't have to be early risers?"

"Sometimes, when there's stock to look over and value—but I got nothing tomorrow so I'm off."

My chair was still warm from the blonde's trim

bottom. I leaned forward and squinted at Tiny who stared back innocently.

"Podolack says you invited him to the poker game. How come you told me he invited himself?"

He frowned thoughtfully. "I told you like I remembered it. He probably didn't want to make you think he was a pushy fella so he remembered it different."

"Okay, tell me again what was said, from the beginning."

"Well, I was sitting up there at the bar and this fella sat down next to me. I knew he wasn't a regular and he didn't look like a guy from around here and so I tried to make him feel at home."

"You started the talking?"

"Sure. I asked was he a stranger in town and he said yeah and we chinned about Fino's. He liked it. And how hot it'd been for days. He said he'd figured South Dakota'd be cooler than where he came from."

"He say where that was?"

Tiny's eyes slipped away from me for a moment as he looked across the room. I glanced around and saw the small blonde going out the door behind an older man.

"I don't think he said exactly where he came from," said Tiny. "I got the notion it was East somewheres. He was real vague."

"And you didn't ask?"

"I might have, I don't remember everything we said. I talk to lots of guys, you know, its easy to forget what they say. I suppose I don't always listen too hard."

I stared at him, but he didn't squirm and then the waitress came over to say it was last call, did we want another. Tiny said yes and she went away.

"Did you talk about Trixie?" I asked.

His mild blue eyes blinked at me. "Trixie?"

"Yeah. Bernie's wife, remember?"

"Of course, but why'd you think I'd talk about her to a stranger?"

"I guess because he told me you did."

He shifted, making his chair creak and his broad face looked hurt and confused. "Are you sore at me, Carl?"

"Why'd I be sore at you?"

"I don't know. Unless you figure I did something wrong. It seems like maybe you're trying to trap me into a lie or something. I wouldn't lie to you. Like I said, I talk to lots of guys. Nobody remembers every little thing they say when they're sitting at a bar having a little drink."

He was so worked up it seemed like he might cry and I butted in. "Don't get excited. I'm just trying to find out what happened. I want to know if this Podolack guy came in here knowing he'd find you and wangled an invitation to the poker party. I'm trying to make you remember what you said because it could be important. Okay? So who brought up Trixie, and how come?"

He took a slow sip of beer, put the bottle down, burped gently, and licked his thick lips.

"Did you tell him Trixie was your girl?" I asked.

He looked horrified. "Of course not. Why'd I lie like that?"

"Come on, Tiny, guys lie about women all the time. Makes them feel good. Makes other guys feel good and like you better. And what the hell, how'd he learn different if he hadn't been invited to the poker game?"

The waitress delivered our beers and Tiny finished his other bottle, pushed the empty toward her and pulled the full one into his meathooks. All that showed of the bottle was the mouth and top inch of the neck.

"I guess I might've talked about her a little," he confessed. "I think about Trixie a lot, you know. It's hard not to talk about somebody you think about all the time."

"Did you tell Podolack you'd laid her?"

He stared at me. The blue eyes were no longer hurt and defensive. "If he told you that, it's a lie. I never said any such thing."

"He didn't say it out flat. But he let me know you tried to make him think so."

"He's a damned liar."

"Okay. But she kidded you a lot, even flirted, right? You always got a lot of attention from Trixie."

The eyes gentled again. "Sure, she liked to tease me because I blush easy. That's always tickled her. I never took it to mean anything. She was just friendly and kind of affectionate."

"Just like I figured. You're old friends and she trusts you."

"That's right. She trusts me, and maybe you. She's real impressed by you, you know."

"No, I didn't know. She never flirted with me."

"Well, no, of course not. Bernie wouldn't have stood for that. And anyway, you weren't around that much."

"You telling me Bernie could be jealous?"

"Of course. Didn't you ever notice? He never offered her to any guys like you or Gene Healey."

"I don't remember him offering her to Ike."

"Oh, Ike, he's too old. She never teased him."

"How about Joe?"

"No. Sometimes she called him Andy Gump. Trixie can be kind of mean sometimes—it's not Joe's fault he's sort of chinless and skinny."

"What'd she call you?"

"Mostly Tiny. Sometimes, when she was sore, she'd call me Fat Atlas. Only a couple times."

"You think Joe ever had her?"

"No. Bernie was more likely to offer her to guys who could do something for him. You know, guys with money or connections. He teased Joe along, now and then, but even Joe knew he never meant it."

"So Joe didn't have too much reason to be nuts about either of them, did he?"

"I guess not. But Joe's not a killing kind of man. He's lots stronger and tougher than he looks, but he's not—I don't know how to say it—he just never feels anything strong enough to do anything final."

"How about Healey?"

Tiny shook his head.

"And Ike?"

"He might've once. Now he's too old."

The waitress came around and patted the table.

"Drink up, fellas, I wanna go home."

Tiny downed his beer with one long gurgle. I got up, leaving my bottle almost full.

"You don't want that?" asked Tiny.

I said no. He picked it up, tilted his round head back and put the bottle down empty a few seconds later.

"I'll give you a lift home," I said.

"It's only a little way."

I assured him that made no difference, I wanted to talk some more. He said okay, if that's what I really wanted, and we walked out past a few die-hards not as sympathetic to tired waitresses as Tiny.

"What was Trixie like as a carny dancer?" I asked as we stepped out into the cool night air.

"Oh, she was pretty good. Trixie wasn't really what I'd call a *dancer*, I mean, she didn't do any fancy steps or whirls. Mostly she walked real teasy and bounced a lot. She wasn't a heavy bump and grinder—didn't have the balance for it—like some can just carry on like crazy and never lose a beat but that's harder to do than you'd think. I've seen beginners stumble and stagger when they were trying too hard. Guys liked Trixie cause she liked showing off so everybody had fun. She wasn't wild, her act was careful and made guys feel good."

"Did she have lots of guys?"

"No. Traveling with a show, you don't get to meet many of the customers, and carny guys were mostly too rough for her. Trixie always wanted a fancy fella."

He tilted my Model T when he climbed in, sat down carefully, and sighed.

"As far as you know, Bernie was her first big moment?"

"Uh-huh. They hit off quick. She quit the show that fall and went back East. I think there was somebody in her family sick. She and Bernie kept in touch and then he went out there and brought her back."

It was just three blocks to his place. He had the lower floor of a duplex. It was a tall, narrow house, set between others of its kind, all white with full width screen porches.

I parked in front and Tiny sat, lost in thought for a moment. Then he turned his round head and asked would I like to come in for a drink.

I said okay and followed him up the walk. A tawny cat, almost as big as a terrier, met us at the front door and meowed with gravel tones.

"That's Teddy," said Tiny. "He's a talker."

He was also a rubber and archer. He banged into my shins hard enough to stagger me and arched his back up for petting so far I could damned near rub his fur without bending over.

We went inside through an entry area where there was a closet and a stairway, made a right and Tiny turned on a lamp which showed a small living room and a dining room beyond. The brown furniture sagged, I assumed from Tiny's poundage, and the arms of an easy chair had been shredded by Teddy's claws.

We walked on through to the kitchen. The floor creaked under his weight and the cat trotted ahead, meowing in time with his steps.

"I used to keep him outside nights," said Tiny as he lifted a gallon of moon from under a curtained counter, "but he learned to climb up on the screen and sway back and forth so it slammed and made such a racket I let him in."

"Why didn't you latch the door?"

"Hell, he'd have torn the screen loose if the door wouldn't give. Anyway, he never messes and I like him around. He's better company than lots of wives I hear about."

I suspected Teddy couldn't cook, but, then, I've known wives who couldn't either.

"He looks like a big eater," I said.

"Sure is. Probably eats more than I do."

Tiny got glasses from an upper shelf, set them on the counter and sloshed clear moonshine into them from a golden-yellow can.

"Want water?" he asked.

"About half."

He went to the sink, added water to my glass and handed it over. The hard South Dakota water smelled of sulphur and hid the scent of alcohol. I took a sip. It was about as smooth as a rusty hacksaw.

Tiny took his uncut moon to the enamel-topped table by the kitchen window and sat down. I sat across from him and stared into the uncurtained window which reflected our images. We looked like a beardless Santa Claus and one of his skinnier elves sitting in a big kitchen. Teddy hopped up on Tiny's lap—or I should say, his fat thighs since his belly didn't leave a lap.

"Did you know Bernie was peddling hot jewelry?" I asked.

"Uh-huh. He offered me some once. Bernie was always selling."

"You buy any?"

"Who'd I buy jewelry for?"

"How about that blonde I saw you with in the speakeasy?"

"She wasn't with me, she's just an old friend."

"She didn't look so old to me. Was that her boyfriend she went out with?"

"I didn't see her go."

"You don't know her boyfriend?"

"She's got lots of friends."

"Ah."

"I didn't mean it that way. She's just real popular. I couldn't say who she was there with."

"She just sat down to say hello, huh?"

"You kind of keep at me, don't you, Carl?"

His blue eyes were beginning to take on a glazed look and they didn't avoid me as much as they had earlier. He kept one huge hand on his glass and kept the other down cradling Teddy to keep him from slipping off.

"Maybe so," I admitted. "It's just that you seemed to know Trixie and Bernie better than anybody else."

"Ike knew them just as well. Knew Bernie longer."

"And liked him even less?"

"I never said I didn't like Bernie."

"You thought he treated Trixie okay?"

"*She* thought so. She stayed with him, didn't she?"

"Right to the last."

He took a healthy swig from his glass, licked his thick lips and looked down at Teddy. The cat blinked and meowed. Tiny meowed back. It was such a good mimicking job I almost thought Teddy was a ventriloquist.

Tiny grinned and peered across the table at me.

"You probably figure I been living alone too long."

"No, I've met lots of folks that talked to animals. Ma talks to dogs—or did when Pa kept them."

"But she didn't bark, did she?"

I admitted she hadn't.

"There's a difference." He stroked the cat and got him purring.

"How'd Ike feel about Bernie messing with his daughter?"

Tiny gave a massive shrug. "He didn't like it. But I tell you, if Ike was going to kill Bernie, he sure wouldn't have done it with a pillow."

"How'd you expect he'd feel about Trixie taking the blame?"

I was a little surprised when he took time for thought before answering.

"Well," he said at last, "out of the four of us, I guess Ike liked her least. Lately it was pretty plain. I remember a few years back, when Trixie and Bernie were first married, Ike came right out and asked her why she put up with what Bernie pulled. She'd just laugh and say, 'Oh, well, you've got to understand Bernie.' Ike said he already did and that told him plenty about her."

"How'd she react to that?"

"It flustered her, but she just put it down to him being a cantankerous old man. Trixie never stayed made at anybody much."

"How'd you happen into the carny business?" I asked.

He laughed, nearly dumping Teddy who woke and grabbed Tiny's leg with all ten claws. Tiny grunted, came to his feet and let the cat drop to all fours. For a second they glared at each other, then Teddy sat down, heisted his hind leg and started a wash job.

"You got no manners," scolded Tiny. After a couple more seconds of scowling he went over and got the moonshine can. I hadn't hardly dented my drink, but he topped it off and filled his own glass, set the gallon can on the table and plunked down in his chair again.

"About joining the carnival," I reminded him.

"It was real simple. I was sitting in a saloon—this was before prohibition—and I bent a silver dollar in half and this fella watching asked what else could I do. I told him to step on my hand. He said, 'Huh?' and I put my hand on the floor and he stepped on it and I lifted him up and put him on the bar. He didn't weigh but a couple hundred pounds—probably less—but he thought that was something and he asked how'd I like to do a strong man act in his show. I figured he was drunk and he was, but he did have a show and the regular strong man had got a hernia and stayed somewheres in Ohio. So for three months I was lifting stuff—mostly girls—and bending railroad spikes and iron bars."

"How come you quit?"

"Well, I just looked fat, not strong, and everybody thought what I did was faked. Lots of it was, of course, just about everybody fakes at least half what you see in a carny show so ordinarily it don't matter.

For me it was different because most people who go for strong men just want to see muscles roll and bulge, it's sort of like a girl making her breasts bounce, you know? So they got a new fella, called the Little Giant. He couldn't have lifted a decent sized watermelon, but you could see every muscle he had from his little toe to his thick ears. He wasn't as tall as you."

"So you took on the girly show barker's job?"

"Yup. It was kind of a comedown but not so sweaty. And it was fun being with the girls."

I asked him more than I wanted to know and he told me more than I could remember or care about and kept on drinking. It looked like he planned to polish off the gallon of moonshine which was near fresh when he started. Every now and then he'd ask if the stuff was too rough and I'd say it was fine and he'd top my glass off again.

Pretty soon his eyelids got heavy and he gazed at me through slits.

"Well," he said, "you finding out what you're after?"

"You don't figure I'm here just to be sociable, huh?"

"You're just sucking the edge of your glass. You used to be a boozer, I know. Most guys hit it like you did, they either quit cold or wind up with snakes."

"I just eased off a little. Tired of jails and all that."

"Getting old."

"Grown up, Tiny."

He shook his head, turned the glass with his thick hand and let his eyes close for a moment.

"Why don't you sack on the porch?" he asked. "There's a cot out there I use when it's too hot to sleep inside."

I grinned at him. "You want to talk some more in the morning?"

"I don't wanna talk anymore tonight."

"You're a very thoughtful guy, Tiny."

"Yeah, that's what all the girls say."

He drank off his glass, stood up, lurched once and Teddy moved swiftly to keep from getting squashed.

After showing me the bathroom and leaving me with a face rag and a towel, he wandered off. Ten minutes later I was stretched out on the cot with thin blanket sheets top and bottom. There was no pillow and I thought it might be just as well, there'd be nothing handy to smother me with if Tiny took the notion. Of course he could always bring one with him. I probably worried about that for half a second before corking off.

A big-mouthed bird woke me. He was perched in a pine tree just outside the porch and there wasn't enough light to give him anything to holler about, but he went at it strong. Then, as if he suddenly came to that it wasn't light yet, he shut up and there wasn't a sound in the world I could hear. Not a cricket, a breath of air or an owl's hoot. I sat up slowly. The cot creaked in tune with my back. I heard something from inside the house.

"No," I thought, "no matter what, Tiny wouldn't murder me on his own porch." Of course if he did, he'd have no more trouble moving me out than in lifting his cat.

Slowly I settled back. Something was on the porch with me. Black as it was, I couldn't believe anything Tiny's size wouldn't show and God knows he couldn't move on that floor without making it creak.

When something landed on the cot I did a backward somersault to the floor and as I came to my feet heard a querulous "Meow?"

Even before his question it had dawned on me who the visitor was and I felt like a damned fool. I moved around, felt for and found Teddy, sat down beside him and scratched between his ears. He began to purr. I stretched out again and he lay against me, purring like a Packard engine. It worked like a lullaby.

Chapter 16

Tiny fed me eggs, bacon, toast and coffee, and no conversation, which suited us both fine for the time. When I finished my fourth cup of coffee and told him I'd better move out, he nodded, frowned a little and raised his hand.

"You know I didn't kill him, don't you?"

"The more I mess with this thing, the less sure I am of anything."

"You'd save yourself a lot of trouble if you forgot about me. I just ain't that kind of guy."

"I'm about convinced."

"Uh-huh. But last night you figured it was me. That's why you stuck around waiting for me to get drunk. You thought I'd admit it."

"It seemed possible. Anyway, it was a good night."

He grinned wide. "See you around . . ."

It was after noon and the police station was hotter than the Kaiser's corner in hell when I arrived.

Sergeant Wendtland, sweating in his shirtsleeves, told me Rita was already visiting with Trixie so I sat and chinned with him while waiting. He said Trixie had settled down some; Howie'd arranged to have better food brought in and the chief had agreed to let her have her own sheets and blankets on the cot with her own pillow.

"She wanted to have her own bed brought over, but the chief wouldn't hold still for that."

"I'm surprised."

"So was I." The sergeant grinned. "If there wasn't so much traffic around here, she might have managed."

"How's Trixie treating Howie?"

"Six ways from Sunday. Whatever'll keep him jumping."

I rolled a cigarette and after lighting it caught the sergeant grinning at me.

"What's so funny?"

"It cracks me up," he said, "you being a regular visitor to the pokey. Doesn't that seem funny to you?"

"Not at all. It's my home away from home."

"Maybe we'd ought to get a cot for you too."

"Don't bother."

"You ever think of being a cop?"

I said no a little too strongly and he scowled. "Why not? What's wrong with being a cop?"

I knew better than to tell him. "Too much discipline," I lied. "Too many hobbles."

"You gotta toe the line," he admitted. "It can be a pain in the ass."

Rita came out of Trixie's room, brightening the gloomy hall like a shot of sunlight. I got up to meet her.

"How'd it go?"

"Let's get out of here," she said. "I'm roasting."

She looked cool in her crisp white dress, even though there were beads of sweat on her forehead and she dabbed at them with a white, monogrammed handkerchief.

I waved at the sergeant and he winked as we took off.

"My God," she said when we were out on the bright street, "we've got to get her out of there."

"Did you learn anything?"

"No—maybe—I don't know. I want some iced tea."

We hiked over to the Cozy Café and took a booth far from the sunny front windows.

The fat waitress showed up, moving slow so as not to work up any more sweat. I ordered two iced teas and she went away, looking abused because Rita hadn't spoken to her.

I watched Rita's face and decided I particularly like small noses with neat round nostrils. If she'd had a long nose with tight nostrils I'd have thought that was classy and enjoyed it, but Rita looked sexy, robust, frolicky, and intent and that got me at the moment. With me, proximity is the greatest charm.

"You're a hell of a good-looking woman," I told her.

"A hell of a lot of good it does me these days."

Her blue eyes met mine and she looked about as flirty as a cop watching a lineup.

"What's the matter—you and Trixie have a fight?"

"Where'd you go last night?" she demanded.

"Back to Fino's."

"And got drunk?"

"I talked with Tiny. Took him home."

"You were going to call me."

"Well, he doesn't have a phone."

"For all you know those two gorillas I got off your

back may have been raping and murdering me and you couldn't even find time to call."

"Hell, Rita, you put Chuck out of business for at least a night, I knew you'd be okay."

"You never gave me a thought."

"The hell I didn't. I was trying to earn my pay. That's how I do it, talking to people."

"And getting drunk."

"I didn't get drunk."

"You weren't drinking?"

"Never emptied a glass."

I was beginning to get sore. The trouble was, I *had* forgotten she might be in danger. All my attention had been on Tiny because I'd decided he was the answer and I can't handle too many notions at the same time.

"So what'd you learn?"

"He's nervous."

"That must've been helpful."

"It was, in a way. He drank like a camel and I thought maybe he was working up to unloading, but all I found out is he thinks maybe I figure he killed Bernie and he's trying like hell to convince me otherwise."

"Did he offer any alternatives?"

"If anything, he tried to get rid of them. He's quite a guy. I slept all night on his porch. It was his idea."

"Did you feel safe?"

"As a baby," I lied. "Tell me what you got from Trixie."

"A lot of nothing." She looked up when the fat waitress arrived with our iced tea, said thanks with a smile and made the poor girl redder than turkey wattles.

"The trouble," said Rita as I dumped sugar into my tea, "is that Trixie is a lovable sister but a dumb broad. She's got herself convinced no jury is going to convict her so she's not in any real trouble."

"Have you talked with Howie?"

"What for? He's so nuts about her he's lost any sense he ever had, which probably wasn't much to start with. Where'd you dig him up?"

"I didn't have a lot of choice."

"There's got to be more than one lawyer in South Dakota. Anybody'd be better. Talk about callow youth!"

I seldom do.

Rita scowled as I stirred the sugar, making the ice clink around. I think it's a nice sound, but people who don't use sugar are very intolerant of those who do. I quit while there was still sugar in the bottom and took a sip. It was bitter.

By the time we finished drinking her mood was a little better and we discussed the notion of talking with Trixie again.

"I'll just lay things out flat, really tear into her her," I said. "Maybe I can jolt her awake."

"I'm ready to try anything, including a rubber hose."

So back to the station we went. As we approached his desk the sergeant glanced up and said, "Hey, Carl, I got a message for you."

"From who?"

"Joey Paxton, the Corden cop. He says there's been trouble at the hotel. You're to come a-running."

"What kind of trouble?"

"Somebody beat up your nephew and smashed the place. They want you bad."

I turned to Rita. "Try talking to Trixie again. I'll call you when I find out what happened."

Her face was all sympathy and concern. "Of course, let me know . . ."

Chapter 17

The road from Aquatown to Corden is just thirty miles but it was far enough to make me sweat. Mostly I thought of Hank, my too good-looking, too smart nephew who'd never, as far as I could remember, made an enemy in his life. I pictured him with a busted snout like mine and a face full of store teeth.

Joey Paxton was sitting in the lobby with Pa when I charged in. Joey looked hangdog, as usual. Pa was red mad.

"This is your doing," Pa yelled at me, jerking his gray head. "Those guys were looking for you."

"Who were they?" I asked Joey.

"They beat Hank and tore up your room and went through my safe," yelled the old man.

"Okay," I told him. "Just let me get the damned story from the beginning. Only first, where's Hank?"

"I had Dave Purcell take him over to Doc," said Joey. "He's okay, just sore and awful mad."

"It's just lucky they didn't kill him," raved Pa.

Finally I got all the story from Joey. Hank had been alone in the lobby when two men came in and asked for me. Hank told them I was out of town. The taller man asked which room was mine. The shorter man stood by the door. Hank asked what difference did it make which was my room, I wasn't in it. The tall man smiled, friendly like, and said they were old buddies who wanted to pull a gag on me.

Hank said he was my nephew and maybe he'd heard me talk about them, what were their names?

"My name's Stuckey," said the tall man. "This is Chuck."

Hank said he'd never heard of either of them. The shorter man walked over, slapped a hammerlock on Hank, lifted him almost clear of the floor and the tall man said he guessed Hank had better tell which room was mine before Chuck broke his arm. Hank hesitated and Stuckey told him if he wasn't helpful they'd just go through the whole place, tearing up every room. Hank gave in. They took him upstairs and he watched while they dumped the bureau drawers, tore the bed apart, cut the mattress open and even peeled off loose wall paper to check the walls. Then they hiked Hank downstairs and, luckily for him, tried the safe door before trying to make him tell the combination. The door wasn't locked and they went through the junk inside. The short guy wanted to take the little cash and a cigar box of Indian head pennies, but his tall partner said forget the chicken feed. Then Stuckey told Chuck to leave me a message and Chuck beat Hank until he dropped. It must not have taken long, he only got a pair of black eyes, one bruise on the jaw, and a cracked rib.

Stuckey had told Hank it was nothing personal.

"Who's gonna pay for the mattress all torn up?" demanded Pa.

"Eventually, a guy named Chuck," I said.

"Meanwhiles, you can sleep on the springs."

"Thanks, but I won't be here. I got to get back to the city."

"What's going on?" asked Joey.

"You're not going to believe me."

"Give me a try." He can look so patient and put-upon he makes me feel like a pup with diarrhea.

"The guys who came here were into something with Bernie Cook. They might've been the killers but right now I doubt it. They tried to take me for a ride last night. They knew I had some jewelry Bernie's girl friend handed over."

"So they were hunting for that. Where is it now?"

"In my car. I'm taking it back to town to see if it's worth anything. I'll have to give it to Baker eventually."

"You get it to him today," he said.

Hank came in, trying to swagger. He was proud of the tape on his cut lip, his half-closed purple eyes, and the sling on his right arm.

I asked how he felt.

"Like I lost."

"This guy that did it, was he fast?"

"Not like you—but tricky. He reached out just like a fellow going to shake hands and the next thing I knew he had my right hand up my back between my shoulders. He didn't break my arm, though. Doc put on the sling because I got a strained muscle in the shoulder."

"Why in hell didn't you take him to my room when he first asked?"

"Well, he just wasn't the kind of guy you want to do favors for."

"He's the kind you don't want to make mad."

"I figured that out after a while."

"I wish I'd been here," said Pa. "I'd have shown 'em."

God knows he'd have tried. Just beause he's over seventy and couldn't hit a wall with his .32 from a yard away, why be shy?

"Did these guys talk while they went through the room?" I asked.

"The chunky one said he'd break my back if I made a run for it. I'll tell you, he could really hit."

"Where'd he slug you first?"

"In the belly. About cut me in half. When I doubled up he kneed me in the face."

So he'd paid Hank back for what I'd handed him the night before.

"You think they'll come back?" asked Hank. It wasn't a question asked in idle curiosity.

"Not if I find them."

"Don't go calling alone," he said.

Boswell, who has the greatest grapevine line in Corden, showed up at my room door just as I was trying to figure out where to begin the salvage job. He was puffing from the strain of climbing the stairs and I picked up my straight chair and got him parked in the hall where he could supervise without being in the way. He watched with sorrowful eyes.

"How's Hank?" he asked.

"Aged some since yesterday."

"Nothing broke?"

"Not anything that shows."

He dug out his stinking pipe while thinking that over. "Why'd you say that?"

"He asked if I thought those guys would be back."

"You think he's scared?"

"Sure, but it's not like him to admit it."

"Mebbe he figures they'll come and this time he'll be ready."

"Not for a while, he won't."

He nodded and concentrated on getting his pipe filled and lit. That took all of his attention. I got the footlocker upright and repacked, folded the sheets and blanket, got the drawers back in the bureau with all their junk, including my emergency moon ration. Boswell spotted that but said nothing so I knew he was taking the whole situation very seriously.

When I had everything taken care of, I stood and stared at the mattress which lay on the bed springs, ripped, gutted, and dripping its stuffings onto the floor.

"That'll be hard to fix," said Boswell.

"Like Humpty Dumpty. And I can't even make an omelet."

I sat on the only unruined corner of the mattress and looked around the tiny room.

"The trouble," I told him, "is that I'm not getting any damned where on this case. It'd be nice to figure these two hoods are the ones who did in Bernie, but it just doesn't add."

"How old are these bully fellas?"

"Hell, I don't know. Thirties I'd guess. Stuckey may be older. What's that got to do with anything?"

"Maybe one of 'em was stuck on Trixie."

"So why'd he try to frame her?"

"She coulda hurt his feelings."

I thought that was too wild but realized it was a possibility. Almost everything mates, or wants to.

"Did you hear the one about the cross-eyed snake?" I asked.

He shook his head.

"The rascal raped a rope."

He looked blank. "What made you think of that?"

"Guys like Chuck mating."

"Fella sounds more like a badger then a snake."

"Yeah. Remind me not to tell you any more jokes, okay?"

Elihu came down the hall and announced that some woman wanted me on the telephone. His tone let me know that no woman ever called a man for a legitimate reason.

I followed him downstairs and went into the booth under the steps.

"Hi," I said.

"You were going to call and tell me what happened," said Rita. She sounded more impatient than mad.

"Yeah, well, things still aren't quite sorted out here. Chuck and Stuckey showed up and my nephew didn't have a girl friend with a loaded purse so he got the worst of it. Nothing broken except maybe some spirit. My mattress got murdered."

"You think they expected to find you there?"

"Either that, or they wanted to leave a message."

She was silent for a moment. "Listen, I got to thinking last night. I don't much like the idea of those two coming around to see if you passed the contraband my way."

"Contra-what?"

"Illegal goods, you know."

"Boy, for an entertainer you've got some fancy words."

"I think you should get back here and bodyguard me. You aren't much of a private detective; I'd ought to get something for my money."

"How about a little entertainment?"

"You're mixed up. I don't buy that, I sell it."

"Are you really worried? You don't sound worried."

"Well, think it over, bright boy, shouldn't I be?"

I didn't have to think long. "Okay, I'm on my way. Keep your door locked and don't open it unless somebody knocks with a shave and a haircut, leaving the six-bits off."

"Nonsense. I'll be down in the dining room. Wear a clean shirt, okay?"

I went back to my room, explained to Boswell that duty called and I had to scoot. He nodded serenely, tucked his dead pipe into a side pocket and ambled off. One of the great things about him is he never says good luck, be careful, or why.

Before putting on a clean shirt I decided on a quick shower. There wasn't time to heat water so I took it straight and was on the road in ten minutes.

"You took long enough," said Rita when I sat down at her table in the dining room.

"Stopped to wash the car, so's not to disgrace you."

"We're not going anywhere I know of."

"Can't be too sure."

She waved the waiter over and I ordered apple pie and coffee.

"You'll never grow up to be big and strong on that kind of diet," she told me.

"There's got to be somebody around to buy small sizes."

"Did they hurt your nephew badly?"

"They didn't do him any good. I'm just glad they didn't treat him like they did my mattress. I had to bury that."

She patted her red lips with her napkin and grinned at me.

"You don't look anything like a scared lady," I said.

"You're here, I don't need to be scared now."

She was wearing an emerald green outfit and looked like a jewel, only better because I knew she was soft.

"Did you bring a whole steamer trunk full of clothes?"

"You think I overdress?"

"You look better every time I see you. Can't wait for tomorrow."

"I'll be wearing another white outfit."

"Great. How're we going to handle this body-guarding business? You expect me to sleep across the door to the hall?"

"No. You'll have a cot just inside. I've made the arrangements."

My chin about bounced on my collarbone. "How'd you manage that?"

"With charm and money. The manager's very understanding. Do you have a gun?"

"No."

"What if these men do?"

"We just won't let them in."

"We can't hide in the room all the time."

"I don't know, it sounds pretty good to me."

The waitress brought my pie and coffee and I got busy while Rita polished off a prime rib.

"Okay," she said when she was satisfied. "I'll give you my key. You go up and check the room out while I take care of the bill. I'll be right along."

Feeling slightly like a trained poodle, I followed orders. The elevator boy gave me a suspicious look, but I stared him down. There was no one loitering in the hall on the fourth floor and I unlocked the door, flipped on the light and gawked around. It was a lot fancier than my cell at the Wilcox Hotel. A closet bigger than my room opened on the right and on the left was the bathroom with a big white tub on claw feet and a toilet fancy enough to double as a throne. The room beyond had flowered wallpaper, eight-foot-high windows, white curtains and brown drapes. A dark green chaise longue, two matching easy chairs, an oak desk, and a bureau gave the place a look of a parlor. The bed was on a little platform and obviously was meant for special ceremonies.

The folding cot had been set up at the foot of the bed and was neatly made up, complete with a white crocheted cover and a huge pillow in a linen case.

There was no one hiding in the closet or under the bed and I checked the window to make sure we didn't have a fire escape for mug access. The street, four floors down, was peaceful. Only a long rope or a tall ladder would get anyone in.

A brisk knock on the door turned me around and I walked over and said, "Yes?"

"It's me," said Rita.

"I don't think there's enough room for you in here."

"Quit clowning and open the door."

"Yes, boss."

She came in briskly, sighted the cot and started to laugh.

"It gives me the feeling," I said, "of being put in my place."

"You mean at my feet?"

"Yeah."

"Does that burn you up?"

"It does if that's what you're trying to do."

"It never occurred to me. Did you bring a toothbrush?"

"No," I admitted. "It never occurred to me."

"You'll find a spare in the bathroom. It's blue. There are also pajamas. Do you have a razor?"

I showed her my World War kit with the take-apart safety razor and blades in an olive drab canvas case.

"What? No shaving mug and brush?"

"Use regular soap, get it hot and wet, spread it, works okay."

She laughed again, patted my cheek and said, "Oh, my hobo bodyguard, you *are* something."

She went to the bureau, pulled the top drawer out and lifted a flask from the right-hand corner.

"Get the glasses from the bathroom," she said. "I'd like about a quarter of water."

"We're going to have a party?"

"Just a sociable drink. There's not enough here for a party."

"I could go scrounge up some more—"

"Uh-uh. We have to be careful. Boogie men, remember?"

I got the glasses, added water to each and brought them out. She poured the moon.

"Mud in your eye," she said, lifting the glass and then took a healthy swig. I followed suit and we grinned at each other.

"God," she said. "What a pair we make."

She was sitting in the chaise and looked like an actress between scenes. I perched on the easy chair just to her right.

"You haven't asked if I talked with Trixie," she said.

"I sort of forgot about her."

"You'd better not—not for long, anyway. She admitted she knew about Bernie and the girl—Ike's daughter. I think I got it across that she could be in serious trouble with a jury if they learned about that."

I built a cigarette and she leaned her head back against the lounge, watching with half-closed eyes.

"How'd you come to be an entertainer?" I asked.

"Well, can you imagine me being a schoolteacher, housemaid, or secretary?"

"Why not?"

"Come on!"

"Okay, so parents wouldn't trust such a doll with their kids, women'd be scared you'd take their men and offices would go to pot. There must be something . . ."

"Not for a woman. Not that pays. I couldn't get a job running a company or an office, even if I was smart instead of good-looking, and nobody would dare hire me for anything I know about without all the town figuring I paid for the job on my back. So I entertain and I'm doing fine. What do they say? May as well have the game as the shame?"

"Well, you've sure given me a new respect for money."

"It takes more than money," she said, and finished off her drink. She kept looking sexier all the time. I began wondering if money-chasing might not be worth trying.

"Where'd you meet the guy you're with now?" I asked.

"At a police station."

"Not me. I meant the guy who's keeping you."

"He isn't keeping me, he supports me. I'm not a damned pet parrot."

"More like a pet leopard. Don't you ever scare him?"

"Nothing scares him. That's one of the things he's got besides money."

"Is he real old?"

"Compared to what?"

"Me."

"I'd guess he could've been your father, barely."

"That's the best way to father anybody."

She laughed, handed her glass over and asked for a refill.

"Do you boss your man around?" I asked as I went over to the bureau for the flask.

"No, I fuss over him. Does it bother you to be bossed?"

"I'm never bossed," I said as I poured moon into her glass. "I just do what I'm asked to when I want to."

She smiled. I went into the bathroom for water and when I returned she was sitting forward looking serious.

"You've had a lot of women," she said. "Have you been careless?"

"You mean, have I had kids?"

"Have you had V.D.?"

"No. Got crabs once."

"I don't suppose you'd be honest about that question."

She noticed I hadn't poured a drink for myself and tilted her head questioningly.

"I'm coasting," I said. "Boogie men, remember?"

"Ah. What'll you do if they fiddle the lock?"

"Have you got an extra pair of stockings?"

"Sure, why?"

"You loan me a pair with two rolls of quarters and I'll fix up a welcome for the boys."

She looked at me thoughtfully for a moment, then drank from her glass, stood up and handed me the drink. I took it and watched goggle-eyed as she pulled up her skirt, rolled her stockings down, held them in her left hand and took the drink back. Then she handed me the stockings, still warm from her legs.

"I'll go get the quarters," she said.

There was one swallow left in my glass. I downed it and fondled the silk in my hands.

A moment later she returned and handed over the quarters.

I fiddled around a moment before getting one stocking into the other, then dropped the quarters into the toe. After wrapping the upper stocking around my fist I hefted the dainty cosh and slapped it into my left palm.

"You'd be better off with my purse, that silk will probably pop."

"It's supposed to be real strong. It ought to last at least a couple swings."

She shook her head. "You should have a gun."

"You've never seen me shoot."

"I bet you'd be good."

"Uh-uh, not with guns."

She walked back to the chaise, sat, pulled her legs to one side and patted the space beside her.

"Sit down."

I did and looked at her. She glanced at the loaded sock I was still holding and told me to put it on the floor.

"What if I need it quick?"

"You'll find it soon enough. I hear you're very quick."

"How come you know so much about me and I can't find out anything about you?"

"You already know too much. And talk too much. Don't you know what to do now?"

I thought I did and we did it, and when she got her breath back she said she'd heard I was quick but this had been ridiculous. I said I was also frequent and she said that might help and it did, but first she made me carry her to the bed. Bossing of that kind is very easy to take.

When we were both tired she went to sleep and I dragged my weary carcass from under the sheet she'd pulled over us and propped a chair against the door. I know you can beat that with a hefty kick if you don't mind noise and have the heft, but I was reasonably sure our playmates preferred quiet.

When I got back to the bed I woke her and took my time. It was very nice and would have been even better if she'd stayed awake all the way.

"My God," she said when we were having breakfast in her room the next morning, "if I stick around here another week one of us will be dead."

I nodded, knowing which one it would be. I didn't really care at the moment.

"Now what are you going to do?" she asked.

I wanted to say "rest," but drank my coffee and looked wise instead.

"I'd better talk with Ike's daughter Adair again. She's probably scared to death and I'm going to have to figure out how to get those gorillas off our back."

"You're tired of me," she said, smiling.

"I'm tired," I admitted, "but not *of* you."

A loud knock made us both jump and for a second we stared at each other before I got up, took the loaded sock off the chaise and moved to the door.

"Yeah?" I said.

"Wilcox, Lieutenant Baker wants to see you. Right now."

"I'll be along in ten minutes."

"I'm to wait for you, sir."

"Wait downstairs, I'll be along."

He said nothing, but the floor creaked outside. With a glance back at Rita, I tilted my head to let her know I was going out and quickly unlocked the door, jerked it open and looked out. A uniformed cop stood beside the elevator.

I turned back to Rita and held out the loaded sock. "He looks real. I'll call you later, okay?"

"Fine," she said, and came over to take the cosh.

"Put the breakfast stuff in the hall and keep the door locked."

She gave me a kiss, patted my cheek and smiled. "Don't get lost."

"Never."

Chapter 18

The cop pressed the call bell as I walked toward him. He was tall, slim, blue-eyed, clean-shaven, and frozen-faced. It was plain he didn't approve of what he guessed had been going on in the room. I felt sorry for him, figuring he'd never have a night in his life like I'd just known.

"How's the lieutenant this morning?" I asked cheerfully.

"Impatient. It's after eleven."

"No kidding. Was he worried about me?"

"Not exactly."

The elevator rose into sight run by a kid even fresher than the one of the night before. He checked to see if I was handcuffed and looked disappointed when he saw bare wrists.

"Down," said the cop.

"No fooling?" said the kid.

The man in blue gave him a stare that made the kid look my way as he started us down. I grinned at him and he nonchalantly palmed his hair back and studied the elevator control lever. He got the floors lined up with only a couple jerks, opened the doors and let us out.

"You really *are* a bum, aren't you," said Lieutenant Baker when I was seated before him.

"Not anymore. I've got a job."

"As a lady's man? You sure don't look the part."

"It's not the part that shows that fills the bill."

"You promised to show first thing this morning."

"This is the first thing I've done this morning, except for breakfast. I didn't promise to come before breakfast."

He stared at me through his sparkling clean glasses and scowled. "So now you're a bodyguard."

"Yup," I confessed.

"Tell me about the threat to the body."

I did.

"Why the hell didn't I hear about this before?"

"Well, it happened after your bedtime. And there didn't seem to be much you could do. I didn't get their address or even the license number."

I expected a rise from that crack but didn't get it.

"You think those guys put the pillow over Bernie's head?"

"Not too likely. They'd have wanted their loot back before knocking him off so they wouldn't be stuck with picking up the loose ends they're chasing now."

"Where are the jewels?"

"Joey's got them," I lied. "For safekeeping."

"Get them back and deliver them here."

"What for?"

"Evidence, what the hell do you think? I'm working on a murder investigation, in case you haven't heard."

145

"I thought you had it all settled."

"Murder's never settled till the trial's over and the appeals are denied. Now bring me the damned jewels."

"Okay, I'll bring them in the morning."

He stared at me for several seconds, tipped his head back and said it better, by God, be before noon. I couldn't figure his tolerance at all and wondered what was going on in his thick head.

"So," he said, "how's your investigation going?"

"Like a grass shack fire."

He told me that was very funny but from now on I was to let him know what was going on or I'd wind up in a cell and now get the hell out he had work to do.

The wind was up when I hit the street, blowing dust and making the few pedestrians squint and hang on to their hats. I walked south to the White Hotel and entered the telephone booth just inside the lobby.

Adair answered on the second ring. Her voice was little more than a whisper.

"This is Carl," I said. "How're you doing?"

She sucked in her breath and began speaking in a panicky rush. "What're you trying to do to me? You want me killed? Why didn't you give them the jewels? I shouldn't have trusted you. How could you?"

"Whoa, keep your shirt on, give it to me a step at a time, okay? What happened?"

"They've been here twice! The first time they listened. I told them Daddy made me give the jewelry to you. They scared me—the short one's just horrible! I gave them the ring right away, I could see them looking at it. Yesterday morning, right after Daddy'd gone out, they came back. The short one was crazy mad. He hit me in the stomach and twisted my arm and jerked my hair. The other one, the older fellow stopped him and talked nice and I gave them the earrings I'd saved to remember Bernard by and then they told me if I didn't get the jewels back they'd do awful things to me and kill Daddy, and they will, you know they will, please, please give them the jewels, Carl."

"Okay, okay, calm down. I held them off the first time because I knew you hadn't given me everything. Now they'll know I've got the rest and they won't bother you anymore."

"You're crazy, you don't know what they're like, especially the short one. He's crazy. He screamed things at me—I never heard anything like that or saw a man who'd treat a woman like he did me. He *hated* me!"

Poor Adair, she was more upset at the idea anyone, particularly a man, could hate her than she was by the beating.

"Does Ike know they were there?"

"I didn't dare tell him. He'd go crazy too. I got sick when the man hit me in the stomach. I had to clean it all up. Carl, I told them where you live in Corden. I told them everything I know or could think of, I was so scared."

"Don't worry about it. Did they say when they'd be back?"

"No. Just that they would be back."

I did what I could to calm her then hung up, went to my car and drove over to Burkhardt's Jewelry. The front windows had been freshly washed, there was water on the sidewalk and dark streaks on the wall under the glass. I opened the door and glanced into the watch repairman's cubicle. Kenny was there, bending over the bench so only his thick, dark hair showed until he looked up. He smiled automatically, and when he recognized me, the smile broadened. I went past the glass partition and leaned my elbows on the counter. He came over and nodded.

"Mr. Burkhardt's not in," he said.

"Expect him soon?"

"No. He's not feeling well. May be in tomorrow. Still looking for used jewelry?"

I shook my head. "Can you give me an appraisal on some I found?"

"How much jewelry?"

"Just a few pieces."

"Something you want to sell?"

"I just want to know what it's worth."

He studied me awhile. He looked strangely content. "It'll cost you five dollars."

"You're a crook, Kenny."

"Aren't we all?" He had a sweet smile.

I told him to wait a minute, went outside, pulled the cigar box from under the seat and returned. Kenny, who was obviously an eager beaver, had returned to his cubicle and looked up at me with the jeweler's scope still in his right eye. He removed the glass and met me at the counter again. I shoved the closed box his way. He looked down without moving his hands toward the box, then glanced up at me.

"Where did these come from?"

"Does it matter?"

"I think maybe yes."

"What are you, Kenny, a fussy crook?"

He smiled. It put dimples in his round cheeks, making him look innocent as a baby. "It'll cost you ten dollars for an appraisal."

I reached over and pulled the box back. "The hell with you."

"I should know where they came from," he insisted.

"I think you know."

"How'd I know?"

"You did business with Bernie."

"So that's where you got them."

"That's where his girl friend got them. She passed them to me for safekeeping."

"All right. I'll appraise them for five dollars."

I shoved the box his way, he took it, pulled it under his face and carefully opened it as if he expected an explosion. A flicker of expression crossed his soft face, but I couldn't guess what it meant. He turned, walked back to the cubicle, got the jeweler's glass and returned. One by one he examined the pieces. He fussed longer than I believed was necessary, but maybe he was trying to give me my money's worth. Finally he straightened up, took the glass from his eye, and shook his head.

"The rings are flawed, the bracelet has little more than commercial stones, the necklaces are very ordinary, and the earrings are baubles."

"So what're they worth?"

"Maybe three hundred dollars, at the most."

I leaned over the counter and he drew back. "You mean that's all you'd offer?"

"That's right." The smile had gone away. He looked worried.

"Do you just buy jewelry when Burkhardt's not in?"

"I don't buy jewelry," he said, drawing himself up. "You asked what I considered a hypothetical question. If it were up to me, that's what I think they are worth. That is, if they weren't stolen. Since I suspect they were, I wouldn't dream of making an offer at any price. You want to give me my five dollars now?"

"You ever deal with a guy named Big Tiny Sorenson?"

"Who's he?"

"A very big man who was a friend of Bernard Cook's."

He shook his head.

"How about Ike Olson? He's a small guy, older than me, younger than your boss. Hawk nose, wild white hair."

"I haven't bought jewelry from anybody. I don't have money to do that with."

"There's nothing in the till, huh?"

"That's all accounted for. It's not mine to deal with."

"Okay. And this five I'm going to give you, does that go into the till?"

"Of course. Now I really should get back to work, okay?"

I dug out his fin, pushed it across the counter, and watched him take it and straighten a folded corner on the glass counter.

"Good-bye," he said. I nodded, took my box and went out. I didn't bother to look back and see if he headed for the till.

A cop was leaning against the front fender of my Model T. It was the same young man who'd come for me at the hotel. He looked very serious and kept his hand on his gun butt.

"Lieutenant Baker wants to see you," he said.

"He already saw me."

"Yeah, I know. He said if you gave me any argument I was to shoot you in the leg."

"He say which one? . . . And that's no argument—"

"Get in your car, we're going to station."

I've generally found that humorless young men can be very dangerous, and this one, having a gun, a billy club, handcuffs, and noble ideals unclouded by imagination, was probably deadly when faced with not being taken seriously.

I said yes sir and did as I was told which was getting to be a tiresome habit. Inside the car, out of sight of the public (which at the moment consisted of one old duffer caning his way along the sunny sidewalk) the cop eased his gun from its holster and pointed it at my bottom rib. Baker had certainly impressed him.

I was marched directly to the lieutenant's office, walked up to his desk and set the cigar box in front of him.

"I just remembered," I said. "I forgot to give this to Joey Paxton so you should have it."

"Very funny. Sit down."

I did.

He stared through his thick glasses and shook his head. "Did you think I was too dumb or too cheap to call Corden and check your story?"

"I thought you trusted me."

"You really think I'm dumb. Suppose you just tell me what the hell you thought you were doing, holding out on me?"

"I wanted to find out what this stuff was worth. And I wanted to check on Kenny's reaction when he saw Bernie's loot."

Baker looked at the cop standing just behind me. I hadn't checked to see if he still had his gun out.

"Kenny's the watchmaker at Burkhardt's Jewelry," explained the young cop.

"How does he figure in this?"

"I got the notion the last time I was in the shop

151

that he might've been dealing with Bernie. Burkhardt said *he* hadn't, and Hadas, the other jeweler, insists he didn't, but it figures that if Bernie was peddling hot ice somewhere he might've found a connection and I pegged Kenny as a probable."

"So what was he supposed to do when he saw the jewels, break down and confess to you?"

"Actually I wanted an appraisal. That's what I went in there for, but when Burkhardt was out, it seemed a good time to check my notion on Kenny."

"What happened?"

I told him.

Baker thought it all over, opened the box, pawed through the pieces, examined the necklaces, and then looked at me through his glasses. Finally he closed the box and shoved it my way.

"Go see Hadas," he said. "Get an appraisal from him. Officer Peterson will go with you and wait outside. Don't sell the stuff and try to duck out the back door. I want you back here toot sweet."

"Am I on the payroll?"

"You pull any more cute stuff on me and you'll be getting room and board out back. Beat it."

Hadas didn't exactly fall all over me but showed interest in the cigar box when I said I was after an appraisal and invited me back to his private office. The fine-looking woman clerk wasn't in sight, but a snooty young guy was and Hadas told him he'd be back in a few minutes.

We sat across from each other over his desk and his dark eyes looked at me, not the box, as he pulled it closer and lifted the lid.

"Where'd you get these?" he asked.

"Take a look, maybe you can guess."

He did. Then he reached for his jeweler's eye,

screwed it in and picked up the top necklace. It had a single pendant and a silver chain. He examined it with more care than I believed it deserved, put it back, lifted out a gold ring with a solitaire diamond, eyed it briefly and then one by one, went through the rest.

"You want to sell these?" he asked, taking the glass from his eye and setting it down.

"They worth buying?"

"That depends on the price."

"Well—" I began, and then a buzzer sounded on the wall behind him.

"Excuse me one moment," he said, got up and went out. He closed the door after him and I followed, edged it open and peeked out. He stopped by the clerk near the front of the store, nodded his head after a couple words and turned around. I was back in my chair when he entered.

"Well," he said, "you wanted an appraisal. I'd guess the pieces are worth roughly $450. That is, if they aren't on record with the police. If they are, they aren't worth a nickel."

He closed the box lid and gently pushed it all my way.

"You didn't happen to recognize any pieces in there, did you?" I asked.

"None of these pieces is distinguished enough to be memorable."

"Like the stuff you used to sell Bernie for his girl friends?"

"Similar." He stood up.

I got to my feet, took the box under my arm and said thanks, I'd be seeing him.

"I doubt it," he said, without a trace of regret.

* * *

I climbed into my car beside Officer Peterson and we drove back to the station.

"While I was in there," I said, "you didn't happen to stroll over and peek through the window, did you?"

"Lieutenant Baker said to keep a sharp eye on you."

He had a sharp eye all right, it matched the point on his head.

We went inside, I gave Baker the loot and described the chinning session with Hadas.

"What do you make of it?" he asked.

"I'm not sure. Like with Kenny, I had the feeling he expected to see something more than he found in the box. He seemed to put off looking inside while he planned how to con me out of believing it was worth anything no matter what. When he actually examined the stuff, he lost interest. I thought that was it even before your friend here gawked in the window and tipped off Hadas's sidekick to the fact somebody was tailing me."

He ignored that crack and frowned thoughtfully. "So maybe the only valuable stuff was the ring you said Adair turned over to them, or the earrings."

I nodded. He glared into the jewelry collection, flipped the lid shut and shoved it away.

"Look," I said, "how about you leave these jewels with me? Then if these guys catch up, I can turn them over and keep Adair and Ike and even me from getting killed."

"Oh, that's a peachy idea. Then, when the jewels disappear, nobody's hurt but old Lieutenant Baker, right?"

"How'd you get hurt?"

"By reputation. Now trot along and peddle your papers, I've got work to do."

"It won't be simpler if one of us gets killed."

"It might if you did."

"You going to have someone watching Ike's place and the girl?"

"I got 'em covered."

"How about me?"

The lieutenant smiled sweetly. "You want I should tell you where you spent last night?"

"Well . . ."

"You were supposed to be on a cot in the White Hotel—only we both know better than that, don't we? You get any sleep?"

"No, I was too busy watching for hoodlums you should've picked up by now."

He told me to hit the road but not leave town and I walked back to the hotel. The tail was obvious. A middle-aged guy in a seersucker suit and scuffed black shoes. When I walked across the lobby to the desk clerk, the seersucker man dropped into an easy chair next to what looked like another cop, probably assigned to cover Rita. It looked like Baker had a whole army at work.

I asked the clerk if Rita was in, he said yes and I went up.

When I knocked, she opened the door a crack and frowned.

"Do I know you?"

"Only in the Biblical sense."

"What do you know about the Bible?"

"It's pretty long and all the people talk funny."

She smiled, opened the door, patted my cheek, and turned to sway-hip her way into the room. Her white silk robe flowed over her like a milk shower. She sat on the chaise where we'd started action the night before and patted the spot beside her. I saw a

155

large vase of red roses on a side table beyond the lounge and took the easy chair a couple feet away.

"What's the matter?" she asked. "Don't you feel cozy?"

"Where'd the roses come from?"

She glanced toward the quarter acre of red and said, innocently, "Oh, those?"

"Yeah, those."

"I didn't think you'd notice."

"I haven't lost my eyesight."

"Are you jealous?"

"Just nosy."

"They're from my old friend. He wants me to come home."

"When're you leaving?"

"It depends."

"Don't tell me—"

"On what happens with Trixie—and you."

"If you go, who'll protect me from Mutt and Jeff?"

"I'd worry about that, I really would."

I moved over and sat beside her.

"Well, I was afraid you were exhausted," she smiled.

"Why should I be?"

"You didn't get to sleep, like I did. What you need is a nice long nap."

"I think I need an encore."

"Later," she said. "Now we have to go see Trixie."

I must have been tired because she was gone before I could move. I watched as she slipped out of the robe and dressed. She moved so quickly I only caught glimpses but it was great and I told her I couldn't wait for later. She went on dressing and was slipping on her stockings when the telephone rang.

"Get it, will you?" she said.

"What if it's your friend asking if the roses came?"

"Tell him thanks, yes."

I picked up the phone and said hello.

"Uh, Carl?" It was Howie.

"Yeah, what do you want?"

"Well . . . " He was obviously embarrassed for me—probably trying to figure out why I'd answer her telephone when my presence in the room would compromise her. "I was expecting to speak to Miss Rita . . ."

"She's getting dressed. What's up?"

"Trixie wants to see her. Is she coming soon?"

"Yeah. Has Trixie decided to confess?"

"Of course not, she just wants to see her sister. When will she get here?"

I glanced at Rita who was smoothing her dress over her hips.

"In about ten minutes."

Trixie's clothes looked a little wilted but her makeup and expression were bright and flashing.

"I just want to talk with Rita," she told me. "I'm sick of talking to men—except Howie of course—but I've already talked too much to him so you fellas take a walk, okay?"

I looked at Howie who stared at her miserably and asked why she couldn't tell him what was on her mind.

"Do me a favor, honey, don't ask, okay?"

So we hiked down to the Cozy Café for a cup. Howie was too owly to talk at first. I wasn't in the mood to coax and we sat in silence, sipping coffee. I smoked.

Finally he sighed, shook his head and leaned toward me.

"I'm not sure but what she should have a different attorney. We're too personally involved, you know? I think she holds back things she is afraid I wouldn't approve of. She can't be absolutely frank and open because of our emotional involvement."

"That big, huh?"

He looked at me soberly.

"You just think it's a physical thing," he said. "That's the way everything is for you. It's different for us. We don't even have to touch. Sometimes we don't even talk."

I didn't say anything and he glared at me, daring me to make some smart crack. I examined my shrinking cigarette.

"She probably wants to talk with her sister about me," he said.

"You're probably right," I said without smiling.

"Don't get sarcastic."

"I thought I was sardonic."

"That's just as bad."

"I thought it might be."

We heated our tonsils and cooled our heels for an hour before Rita came in and joined us. I looked at her—slim, smart, young, and classy—and wondered how it was possible for a guy like Howie to prefer her sister. Well, as Grandma always used to quote the old Indian, if everybody thought alike they'd all want my squaw.

"What'd she say?" demanded Howie, getting to his feet.

"She wanted me to bring her some Kotex."

Howie turned red and muttered something as he sat down.

"That took an hour?"

"Not all of it. We talked about Mamma and other things when we were little. What's the matter, did you get bored?"

"Oh, no. Howie was full of jokes, magic tricks, and fine dance. You should've been here."

"I can see he drew a crowd," she said, glancing around the deserted café.

Howie got up and grumpily let us know he had more important things to do. We watched him hike off, hurt and miserable.

"So what'd Trixie tell you?"

Rita waved for more coffee, got it, and after drinking a little pushed the cup aside and propped her chin on her small fists.

"What Trixie did that night was beat Bernie harder than she ever had before. Then she got dressed, and told Bernie she was going to Podolack's place to spend the night with him. She was wild mad. She told him she knew about Adair. Bernie tried to tell her that he messed with other women because it made Trixie competitive. Well, that made her madder than ever. She told me she had to leave or she really would've killed him. But she didn't go to Podolack, she hadn't liked him at all, he was too chunky and cold. So she went around to Fino's looking for Tiny or Gene—guys that liked her. What she needed was a friend she could unload on, but she's never been good with women and there wasn't one in town she could talk to. Can you imagine what it'd be like not having a soul you could talk to and confide in?"

"Yeah, so what happened?"

"So nothing. She didn't see any of the guys and men that tried to pick her up only scared her. She had a drink and went home."

"And she went straight to bed in the spare room?"

"That's what she still says."

"Okay. So if that's all on the level, somebody had plenty of time to drop in and smother Bernie."

"I know it sounds phony, but she was worried about what everybody'd think—especially you and Howie—if she admitted she'd gone looking for a man."

"If she was really looking for one, why didn't she go where they lived?"

"She didn't know anybody's address."

"Isn't there a phone book in their place?"

"Carl, come on. Trixie's not a practical woman. She just charges off when she's excited, she doesn't think or plan stuff."

"It seems she can plan a story. I don't see where it makes her look any worse to go looking for a guy than sticking around with a louse like Bernie."

She picked up her coffee cup, sipped, and frowned.

"I'll tell you, I don't know when to believe her anymore. She lived with that liar so long it rubbed off, I'm afraid. I just don't see how she can be so dumb. I suppose it comes from Ma, she wasn't too bright either."

I knew better than to agree with her. After a while she looked at me and tilted her head.

"You going to go check at Fino's?"

"Yeah. Want to come along?"

"I don't know if I can squeeze it into my social calendar, wait'll I check—"

"And Howie called me sarcastic."

"I'm not sarcastic, I just try to be funny sometimes. You can laugh if you want."

I grinned and she remained sober-mouthed but her eyes got the arched look of a laugh.

"You want to go back to the hotel?" she asked.

"Hell, yes."

"The only trouble is, everybody'd know."

"So?"

"Well, people don't think so much of it at night, but doing it in the daytime, that could ruin my reputation."

"I didn't think that worried you much."

"It might have a bad effect on you. You're supposed to be a private detective, not a gigolo, right?"

"Gigolo's can dance. That lets me out."

"Okay. Anyway, I'd rather have something to look forward to later."

"You sure know how to keep a man fine-tuned."

"Don't I though?" she beamed.

Chapter 19

                            When we were overtanked on coffee she suggested a walk and I led her down McKinley Street to the riverfront. We stopped on the bridge and stared at the clay-tinted water which took on a gold cast where the sun hit it. Farther south it reflected blue sky and small white clouds.

"We should have been on a picnic," she said. "This is the nicest day I've seen in South Dakota. Hardly any wind and not really hot."

I admitted it didn't seem natural as I turned and leaned my elbows against the railing behind me. Our trailing cops stood on the sidewalk just before the bridge, smoking. Neither of them looked our way.

"Are they supposed to protect us or just try and catch us doing something illegal?" asked Rita.

"Both, I suppose."

A black Buick appeared, coming from the east. It passed the two cops who stared at it blankly as it moved by. We watched idly. Then I recognized the driver.

"Oh-oh!" I said, and grabbed Rita's arm but before we could move two steps the car was beside us.

"Mr. Wilcox," said Stuckey, speaking through the open window, "I'm alone and unarmed. I want to talk with you, please get in."

I glanced back at the cops who were watching but hadn't moved yet. A quick peek in the back seat showed no Chuck so I looked at Rita with raised eyebrows.

"Why not?" she said.

I opened the door, she hopped in, I followed, the cops yelled, and Stuckey put the car in gear and took off. I glanced back, gave the cops a cheerful wave and a moment later we were wheeling along the prairie.

"It was too bad what happened to your nephew," said Stuckey. "I feel real bad about that."

"I wasn't too delighted myself," I admitted.

"You shouldn't have embarrassed Chuck the way you did the night before. He took it out on the boy. I stopped him before he could do any real damage, but that was the most I could do."

"I'm sure God'll understand."

He leaned forward to peer around Rita at me.

"We have to be reasonable, Mr. Wilcox. Businesslike. It just isn't profitable for us to carry grudges and harbor ill feelings."

"I'll try to remember that. What's our business now?"

"Jewelry." He said that reverently.

"Ah."

"You've got it. You gave the young lady a note for us and when we asked for delivery, you refused. Why?"

"Nobody offered a reward for services."

"Well, I can understand that. What do you think would be adequate?"

"How about five hundred?"

I peeked around Rita and saw him swallow hard. He kept his eyes on the graveled road for several seconds, then side-glanced me.

"Exactly what have you got?"

"You passed the stuff to Bernie, you'd ought to know."

"He could've sold some of it. The girl might have held out."

I described what Adair had given me. He drove in silence for a few moments, then slowly shook his head.

"Something missing?" I asked.

"I'm not sure. Did one of the necklaces have any green stones?"

"You mean emeralds?" asked Rita.

"Yes." I thought I heard eager in his voice as he turned toward her.

"I didn't see anything green," I said.

"Ah," he said, and the disappointment in his voice was plain.

Rita looked at me with raised eyebrows, then turned to him. "There was a special necklace in the lot, huh?"

He shrugged casually. "One might have been a little better than the rest. We could probably make a bargain on what's left. How would four hundred sound?"

"Not quite as good as five," I said.

He smiled. "Could we compromise on four-fifty?"

"Why not?"

"I like you, Carl," he confided. "You're a reasonable man. Now then, I've one favor to ask."

He didn't state it and I let him hang as we kept moving along the graveled road between parched fields of wheat and corn. We came to a crossroad and he turned right. I looked out my window and saw the tail of dust behind us, twisting and lifting in the easy wind.

"You talk with Trixie every day, don't you?" he asked.

"That's right."

"Good. What we'd like is that you ask her if she remembers seeing a necklace with emeralds in it. If she happens to know whether Bernie sold it or not."

"What's so special about this necklace?" asked Rita.

"Nothing much, except it was promised to a certain party. A fellow we know who's been a very good friend. It was, you could say, special ordered, see? We wouldn't want to disappoint our friend."

"Are you sure he hadn't already got it?" I asked.

He gave an embarrassed laugh. "Pretty sure."

"Have you asked him?"

He swallowed. "Well, I think you can see that'd be a little awkward. I mean, you don't ask a fellow you're doing a favor for whether you've already done it or not, you know what I mean?"

"I haven't the foggiest notion what you mean. It sounds like you're doing a favor for a guy through some other guy that you can't trust. That's a dumb kind of favor."

"It's a little complicated," he admitted. "The trouble is, this fellow can't afford to have direct deals with us. He's sort of a bigshot. Public figure, you know? Very sensitive business."

"A politician, or a cop?" I asked.

"Better you shouldn't know."

"I'll bet."

"Will you ask Trixie about the necklace?"

"Sure thing. Then what?"

"Let me know what she says."

"Okay, where do I reach you?"

"I'll call you. I can ring the lady's hotel room, okay?"

"And then we turn over the jewels and you dish out the four-fifty, right?"

"Exactly. A good bargain."

I wondered if he had any notion that my offer was as phony as he knew his was.

He took another turn that headed us toward town.

"I think we'd ought to get one more thing from you," said Rita.

"What's that?"

"What do you know about this Podolack guy?"

"Who's he?"

"He was in the poker game at Bernie's Friday night."

"Oh?"

"He'd never played with them before. Big Tiny met him that afternoon at Fino's and brought him along."

"So where'd this guy come from?"

I told him what I knew. He asked for a description. It was impossible to be sure, but his curiosity seemed genuine. He asked did I know whether the cops had grilled him hard and I said I didn't know.

We drove in silence a ways before Rita piped up.

"What I don't understand is how you men got involved with Bernard Cook. Everybody says he was a liar, you've said he was unreliable, but you turned jewels over to him as if he were some kind of wholesaler while he operated in a town too small and poor to have a market for crackerjacks."

"Oh, well, there's always a few people around with

money if the deal's right. Bernie knew lots of people."

"Things must've been too hot for you in the cities," I suggested.

"We did have a little problem Chuck got us into."

"How long have you been teamed up with him?"

He grinned ruefully. "All his life. He's my little brother. I've always looked after him. He's not a bad guy, just a little short on patience and awfully impulsive. Most of the time I keep him pretty reasonable. Well now, we're about back in town. If you folks don't mind, I'll just drop you off a few blocks from the hotel, okay?"

"You think cops'll be looking for us?"

"It seems possible."

"Are you afraid they'll ask you where you were when Bernie got knocked off?"

He grinned harder, showing some gold and a gap behind his right upper eye tooth. "We've no problem there. Weren't even in town and we can prove it."

"So why so shy of the cops?"

"They make Chuck nervous. That brings out the worst in him."

I guessed that could be pretty bad.

When he let us out I leaned down and spoke to him through the window. "I'll find out what I can about the necklace and we'll see if we can deal on the rest. But whatever comes off, keep your little brother off my family."

"Certainly. You help me, I'll help you. Everybody's happy."

"Uh-huh. Clean hands and a clean conscience."

"Absolutely. Chuck was mad, but he's not crazy. He'll accept what I say, given time."

"Fine. Just keep him out of my sight. I'm not all that forgiving."

Chapter 20

"Now what?" asked Rita as we stood on a quiet street and squinted under the bright sun.

"I'm gonna have to talk with Howie."

"Why not Trixie?"

"If we show up at police headquarters right after gabbing with a suspicious character, Baker's going to want all the details. Before I have to unload, I want to see Howie."

She put her hand up to shade her eyes as she peered at me.

"You think Trixie'll be in bigger trouble than ever if they think she's got that necklace, huh?"

The truth was, I wanted time to think and felt uncomfortable about leaving my family alone while little brother Chuck was still nursing a grudge. I nodded in response to Rita's question, took her arm and headed for my car.

"I guess you're taking me along," she said.

"There's no percentage in going alone. I may need protection."

Her grin was warmer than the sun and she squeezed my arm so hard she threw us out of step as I grinned back.

I lost some notion of my self-importance when we found no one in sight watching my car. The letdown was relieved in knowing I wouldn't have to argue with anybody before taking off for Corden.

Rita was silent until we were a couple miles out of town and driving along between scruffy cornfields. The sky was all pale blue, almost white around the sun and darker on the horizons that looked a world away.

"What throws me most," I told her, "is where Bernie planned to peddle jewelry, or why those jokers thought he'd manage."

"Like the man said, there are always rich ones around, even here."

"Maybe, but they're sure not a common breed. Our vices run to sex and gossip."

"And bootlegging."

"That's no vice, that's a profession."

It was near supper time when we wheeled into Corden and I warned Rita that I dassn't take her to the hotel as a surprise because Bertha, the cook, would have a conniption fit.

"The only thing everybody in the Wilcox Hotel agrees on, is you don't rile Bertha. She's meaner than a she-bear with cubs and piles, but she gets tolerated because she cooks good. We'll go by Howie's office and see if he'll go to Gus's place for supper with us."

I parked in front of the white clapboard building with its square-topped false front and we climbed the creaking stairs to the second floor hall only to find his door closed and a sign that said he'd be back in the morning.

I decided he was eating at his boardinghouse so we went directly over to Gus'.

Actually Gus' belongs to a guy named George now. George used to be head cook in an Aquatown diner. When Gus died and his wife Claire went to prison, George showed up with savings, jacked them with a loan and bought the place. He kept the old cook and Rosie so there wasn't hardly a hitch in the operation. He hadn't even got around to changing the sign out front which read, "Gus Gardner's Café."

I escorted Rita into the place which had a counter lining the west wall, booths along the east, and tables between. There were a fair number of yokels present, filling all the booths and leaving only a couple of empty tables. I took the one nearest the kitchen. Rita drew attention from every soul in the joint and guys who wouldn't acknowledge my existence if I showed up alone, all called old-buddy greetings hoping she'd bless them with a glance from her blue eyes. I spotted old Boswell at the counter, nursing a piece of pie and a cup of coffee. He smiled my way, showing his tobacco-stained teeth. I waved him over. He hesitated, then picked up the pie plate, carefully placed it on top of his coffee cup and walked over slowly, holding the works with both paws.

"This is Rita," I told him as he sat the cup and saucer down and removed the plate.

He ducked his head and said, "Ma'am," as I shoved a chair out for him. He sat, wheezing a little, and settled comfortably as if he had just ended a long, uphill climb.

"She's Trixie's little sister," I explained. "This is Boswell. He says Trixie didn't kill Bernie."

"Has he got a following?" she asked.

"Sure. He makes good moonshine so everybody that buys from him thinks he's right about everything."

"Do you sell a lot?" she asked.

"Not a *real* lot," he assured her. Boswell always gives the impression of reassurance, even if you don't come around in a worried state.

She smiled and he blinked as if dazzled.

"She's better looking than Trixie, isn't she?" I said.

"She's awful pretty," he agreed.

Rosie came over to take our orders, glanced at Rita and raised her eyebrows at me. We ordered roast beef and when Rosie was gone Rita asked if she happened to be one of my girl friends.

I said not so you could notice it and she looked unconvinced.

Pretty soon she began trying to pump Boswell a little, asking how long he'd known me and what'd he done before he began making moonshine. Since Boswell is a listener, not a talker, she got short answers politely given and soon decided there was no point in pressing him. When the beef arrived she began eating with her usual efficiency. Boswell made a couple small conversational offerings. He said Trixie was a nice lady and he hoped I'd be able to help her out.

"You think there's much chance he can?" she asked.

"You can depend on him," Boswell said almost firmly.

"I guess I'll have to."

We were ready for dessert when Joey Paxton ambled in, gawked around and strolled our way. I made introductions and he acknowledged them without goggling.

"I got a call from Lieutenant Baker," he said. "He's worried about you."

"Oh?"

"He says you may have been kidnapped this afternoon. A couple of his men saw you getting into a car and nobody's seen you since."

"You better give him a jingle and tell him you have."

"I think you'd better. He sounded like a worried father—afraid because the kid's late but mad because he figures he's up to no good. That fella could land on you with both feet if you upset him enough."

"I got to talk with Howie before I see him."

"Well, I just seen Howie go up to his office. You'd better hustle over there."

I asked Boswell if he'd keep Rita company and he said he didn't mind. I told him to have another pie and coffee, my treat, and promised Rita I wouldn't be long. She said she thought she'd survive.

Joey walked out with me.

"I hope you're not getting into trouble again," he said.

Unlike Boswell, Joey's face would make you worry just when you thought you had the world by the tail with both hands.

"I hope not too."

"I suppose this's got something to do with them fellas that beat up Hank and wrecked your room?"

"Yeah, there's a connection."

"It seems to me I'd ought to know about it."

"Don't worry, I'll tell you. But first let me talk with Howie, okay?"

"I suppose I got as much choice as you usually give me."

* * *

Howie sat hunched over his big desk which had nothing on its surface but a gooseneck lamp and his elbows. His face and all the room was in deep shadows.

"Thinking?" I asked.

"Trying to."

"It looks painful."

He straightened slowly, pulling his elbows off the table.

"I guess you got a problem with Trixie," I said.

"She *is* still in jail."

"Well, it may not help, but I've got something new. Mr. Stuckey talked with me today. Says there's a necklace missing from Bernie's collection. It must be a dandy because Stuckey offered me cash if he can get his mitts on it. His story is that some hotshot's been promised delivery and for all he knows, the thing may have been delivered."

Howie stuck his thumbs in his vest and leaned back. "Why'd he tell you all this?"

"He wants me to question Trixie about it."

"Uh-huh. And while he's at it, he suggests another motive for Trixie to do her husband in."

"I think he really wants the necklace. Somehow I think his neck's on the line if he's lost it."

He didn't ask why so I knew he wasn't paying any real attention.

"He also says that he and Chuck have iron-clad alibis for the Friday night Bernie was killed."

I saw his shadowed head tilt back. "You think you can put any credence in that?"

"I'm not even sure I can believe it."

He sighed. "Why are you always doing the dumb act?"

"It comes natural. So what do we do now?"

"I don't know. Where are the jewels you got from Adair?"

"Baker's got them," I told him.

"Does Joey know what's going on?"

"He knows Baker's looking for me. Baker called him this afternoon and said I'd been kidnapped. Now Joey thinks he's got to let him know I'm in Corden."

Howie wanted to know about the kidnapping. I explained it all and he sighed again, said let's go talk with Joey, turned out his light and locked up the office.

After some talk, Joey agreed to let Howie call Lieutenant Baker about me. It was quite a conversation. Baker was so mad I could hear everything he said. He wanted me back in town at once if not sooner and Howie said there'd be plenty of time in the morning and, in the end, Howie won. It tickled me, this fuzzy-chinned rookie lawyer, keeping calm and talking back to the tough veteran cop. I've noticed that there's nothing tougher than a man with lust in his heart. They win over men in love because they don't mess with idealism.

"All right," said Howie after hanging up, "tomorrow you go back to the city and we'll talk with Trixie. Get a good night's sleep. Baker'll probably try to skin you before noon."

"What do I tell him about Stuckey's talk with me?"

Howie leaned against the wall and pushed out his lower lip until he looked like Jackie Cooper in *The Champ*. Then he sighed, looked at the ceiling, and shook his head.

"We've got to find out more about Stuckey and Chuck, and that can only come from Baker. We can't even be sure the police don't have the necklace already. Tell Baker the truth and see if you can trade that for dope on those two men."

Back in the café, Rita had drawn a small crowd. Boswell was in the chair at her right but two guys were in the other chairs and a third was standing by. They all looked fresh through high school. The one standing saw me first and said, "Oh-oh," as he nudged the husky kid sitting on Rita's left. Everybody looked at me and the kid across from Rita shoved his chair back and stood.

"Well," said Rita. "I was about to give you up and go to a movie."

"Fine," I said, "it'll start in about ten minutes."

"Okay," she said. "Who's taking me?"

She looked at the guys. Only the husky one still at her side managed not to look away. He swallowed and said he would.

Rita caught the mood, glanced at me, and shook her head.

"Thanks, Freddie, I guess not this time. The guy that brung me wants to talk and I'll have to listen."

Freddie gave me a hard look, letting me know I was getting off easy, and got up.

"I've already seen the movie anyway," he said.

"Good," I said. "In that case you won't miss a thing."

He thought that over, trying to decide if he should take offense.

"So long, fellows," said Rita quickly. "It was nice talking with you."

They all smiled at her sheepishly and drifted back to a booth near the front.

Rita stood, picked up her purse and looked at me levelly. "Why do I feel like everybody was just about to explode?"

"Maybe you were in the mood for some excitement."

"You mean you think I was trying to start something?"

I told Boswell I'd see him again soon and he nodded, giving me a look of rare concern.

I paid the cashier and walked out with Rita following closely.

"Are you sore because I was friendly with those kids?"

"Why'd that make me sore?"

"That's what I'd like to know. We were just having a laugh or two and in you barge, looking like an outraged husband catching his wife in bed."

"What you do is your business. And I didn't come in looking like any goddamned husband—I was thinking about the hell I'm going to catch from Baker tomorrow."

Except for a couple of cars angle-parked against the high curb, the street was deserted as a ghost town. A small whirlwind lifted a dust spout in the gravel then dropped it and vanished.

"What's Baker's gripe?" she asked as we walked west.

"He's pretending he's sore because we ditched his tails but what really galls him is that I didn't get bent or broken."

She laughed, took my arm and leaned close. "Are we going to stay in your room?"

"It's only got a single bed."

"So we'll take turns on the bottom."

"You could've caused a lot of trouble back there in the café, you know."

"Uh-uh. I was the one that stopped things. You sure weren't any help, coming on all ugly."

"That Freddie boy, he thinks he's tough. He's the kind that's got to look good in front of his pals."

"That's why I let him down gently. I understand guys, don't worry."

"One time you'll outsmart yourself and get some faces busted."

She jerked me to a halt and pulled her arm free. "Were you actually ready to fight those kids?"

I'd been itching to and that fact made me madder than hell. "They weren't kids. Those were full-grown men—two of them bigger than me."

"I see. So you figured they couldn't take you seriously unless you knocked them down, is that it? Fighting's what makes you feel big, isn't it?"

"Quit hollering, you'll draw a crowd."

"There aren't enough people in this burg to make a crowd, and if there were, so what? You worried about your reputation?"

"That's about the eighth question you've asked and you haven't waited for an answer yet."

"There aren't any answers. You're just a brawler. You don't give a damn for anything but being the town tough. Okay, take me back to my hotel. . . better yet, tell me where I can catch a bus or a train."

She looked meaner than a mad bobcat with her mouth screwed up, her eyes all squinty, and her head pushed forward. I glared back, probably looking twice as mean considering my mug, and came close to saying she should suit herself before I got a little smart and pulled up.

"Okay," I said. "Relax. I'm not that bad."

"The hell you're not." She said it fierce but lowered the tone and for a moment we quit glaring and looked across the street at the weathered white hotel.

"Let's take a walk," I said.

Her mouth softened as her eyes lost their mad squint. When I moved she came along and we passed the hotel, walking west up the long hill under arching elms that lined blocks of squarish white houses.

"Corden has more trees than most prairie towns. I don't know why since we don't have a river or creek. I suppose some time back, folks watered them. Now, with the drouth, they're drying to death."

She shuffled her feet to get in step and looked at me. "You really love this miserable country, don't you?"

"I'm used to it."

She took my hand.

"And you got mad because I didn't take you seriously enough, that was it, wasn't it?"

I shrugged, not wanting to talk about it and she smiled warmly.

"We had a great time last night, didn't we?"

I nodded.

"So why're we wasting time, wandering around?"

"I can't quite picture taking you into the Wilcox Hotel. If I put you in a good room the family'll know and there'll be a hassle. And I wouldn't take you into my room."

"You think I'm snooty or something?"

"I think you're classy and I'd rather not show you what a bum I am."

She moved against me. Her eyes were only a half an inch lower than mine.

"You want to go back to my room?"

"Damn right."

Chapter 21

The second night wasn't anything like the first. She was almost fierce at the beginning but worked it off quickly and then became, for her, damned near tender. She didn't kid or laugh and went to sleep early. I woke in the middle of the night and found her curled close to my back with her arm around me. When I opened my eyes in the morning, she was watching me, her face on the pillow not six inches away.

"You have gentle eyes," she said. "Asleep you look tough. I've always read about how men look younger and innocent when they're asleep but you look tough."

"That just shows you can't believe everything you read."

"It isn't just the nose. There's something in the mouth."

"Yeah, it's unbrushed teeth."

"Partly I suppose it's because your beard is so

dark. Your whiskers are absolutely awful, you know? You should shave just before you go to bed."

"Okay, I'll wait."

She wouldn't settle for that so I got reasonably presentable and after breakfast we went down to the police station. She held on to my arm all the way, saying she needed an anchor against the hot wind that whipped around us and guys we met stared enviously and watched to see if her skirt would lift and give them a view.

Sergeant Wendtland told me Baker was waiting in his office. His tone suggested I wasn't many steps away from the firing squad.

"He want to see Rita?" I asked.

"He wants to see *you*."

So she went to visit Trixie and I entered the lion's den.

Baker shoved a file away as I came in, took off his glasses and folded his thick fingers on the desk, making a large, double fist. His eyes were about as tender as a hawk when it's swooping on a mouse. I was tempted to remark on what blue eyes he had but his expression didn't encourage cuteness.

"You wanted to see me?" I said, sitting down.

He glared for a few seconds, then unwrapped his hands, put his glasses on and asked, "Who was in the Buick?"

"Stuckey."

"Alone?"

"Yup."

"Tell me about it."

"He offered us a ride. I figured, why not? I'd never been in a Buick before."

"Uh-huh. What was he after?"

"He wanted to know what I'd done with his ice."

"And?"

"I let him think I still had it."

"You figured he wouldn't knock you off till he had it back, huh?"

"I didn't think he'd talk to me much if he knew you had it."

He leaned forward, propping his elbows on the desk. "What'd he talk about?"

"He said he and his gorilla had iron-clad alibis."

"Why the hell'd he tell *you* that?"

"Maybe he figured I was such pals with Bernie I wouldn't do business with him if I thought he killed the man."

"Sure. That explains why he beat hell out of your nephew and terrorized everybody in the hotel. He didn't want to make you sore."

"He apologized for that."

"Good. That made everything just dandy, huh?"

"He offered me four-hundred-fifty dollars for the jewels."

He sat back and put his hands flat on the desk edge. "You're bullshitting me."

I shook my head.

"That lot's not worth four-fifty retail, for Christ's sake."

"Maybe it's got sentimental value."

"Uh-huh, and you're a virgin. So what kind of a deal you make?"

"I said I'd take it. Now all I got to do is get the ice back from you."

He grinned. "Okay. Just set him up and let me know where. We'll take care of the rest."

I said fine and got up to go.

"Oh," said Baker, giving me an old-buddy smile, "just one thing more. You lose your tail again and you'll wind up in a cell. Protective custody, you know?"

"Since when has the guy being tailed been responsible for staying tailed?"

"Since yesterday afternoon when you shook my boys."

Half an hour later Rita, Howie, and I sat in the Cozy Café, making like three bolsheviks plotting a bomb toss as we leaned across the table with our heads together. Trixie had told Rita she'd seen the necklace with the emeralds. It had been hidden in Bernie's underwear drawer and she'd guessed it was for Adair. She kept that suspicion to herself until Friday night when she was beating him. He swore it was going to a judge who was buying it for his mistress.

"Did she believe him?" I asked Rita.

"Would you?"

"Hell, no."

"Well, neither did she. When she was tired of pounding him she went to the drawer for the necklace and found it gone. He said it'd already been delivered to the judge and in a day or so he'd have the payment."

"Who delivered it?"

"She didn't think to ask. She was about crazy, you know. She said Bernie was crying and she thought she'd hurt him bad."

"What do you think?" I asked, looking at Howie. He was too discouraged to meet my eyes at first, but finally he did and asked if I'd told Lieutenant Baker about the emerald necklace. I shook my head.

He sighed. "I don't know if that's good or bad. There's no way to know if Bernie was lying or not. Maybe the judge does have it, but for all we know, the police might've found it somewhere in the house when they searched immediately after discovering the body."

"It's even possible that it's *still* hidden in the house, isn't it?" asked Rita.

"No," he said. "The police would've found it."

"Not necessarily. It wasn't as if they had to search for a weapon. All they'd be looking for was something in writing that'd show problems or motives for killing him. I'm for taking a shot at the house."

"You'll be wasting your time," said Howie. "The place will be locked or watched. You'll never get in."

"Well, if I don't lose the tail, they won't lock me up for trying."

Two plainclothesmen tailed us as Rita and I strolled toward Cook's house. When we were just turning in on the front walk, Podolack got out of a Chevvie at the curb and called me. We halted, he approached and stopped so close I could smell his sour breath. His face was expressionless as a window dummy's.

"I want to talk to you," he said.

"Fine. This is Rita, Trixie's sister."

She said hello and didn't get a glance.

"Alone," he said.

"Okay," said Rita. "I'll go up into the house."

Podolack glanced at the tails, who'd stopped to admire the handiest shrubbery, and turned back to me.

"We'll go inside too."

Rita went ahead up the two steps to the porch and tried the door. It wasn't locked. She pushed in and we followed.

Podolack looked back through the door window,

then turned to me, his face still stiff and blank. "What'd you tell the cops?" he asked.

"About what?"

We were standing in a hallway, just before a flight of steps that went up to the bedrooms. On my right, as I faced the front door, was the living room.

"About me," he said.

"I'm going upstairs," said Rita.

"Fine." It occurred to me I ought to ask that she leave her purse but decided that'd sound queer and maybe I could manage okay if I could maneuver us into the living room, which would give me more dodging space.

Rita hiked up the stairs and when Podolack didn't bother watching her legs I knew things were going to get serious.

I moved into the living room and he stayed close.

"I want to know exactly what you told the cops and I want to know now."

"I didn't tell them anything about you. I don't know anything about you."

"I think you're a liar."

"Hey, careful man."

He tapped me with his stubby forefinger about as gently as a cop pushing a billy club.

"I know you're working for that hooker," he told me. "She called you in and you're gonna stick that killing on anybody but her—"

"Don't poke me again."

His finger jabbed the same spot, right under the collarbone.

I've never found much percentage in debate with a hot-head or in working up to a fight with a lot of pushing and yelling. So I feinted a left to the head, hooked him with a right to the gut, and as he doubled, whipped over a rabbit punch. He should have dropped but was too dumb to know it and stumbled forward, trying to bearhug me. I skipped to his right and caught him with a right where the neck and shoulder meet. He switched direction, crashed into the brown couch and bounced to the floor.

I was standing just beyond easy reach when Rita popped through the door, clutching her trusty loaded purse with both delicate hands.

She stared at me, glanced at Podolack and leaned casually against the door jamb.

"What made me think you'd be the one on the floor?"

"Can't imagine. Find anything?"

"No, I heard the fracas before there was time. Came to the rescue."

Podolack pulled himself together, wondering why his right arm was nearly paralyzed.

"What'd you hit him with?" asked Rita.

"A rabbit."

"He must've been petrified. Can you stay peaceful if I go back up?"

"Ask him."

She walked over and knelt down beside him.

"You okay?"

Podolack tried to lift his right hand, grunted, let it drop, tilted his head back, and for a moment looked like he wanted to touch the ceiling with his chin.

"He fouled me," he complained.

"I wouldn't be at all surprised. I hope you're not going to try and get even for a while."

He slumped back against the couch and wearily shook his head.

"I'll be right back," she said, and took off.

I sat down in an easy chair opposite Podolack. "I

185

really didn't tell the cops anything about you. What'd they ask that made you think I had?"

He closed his eyes and grimaced. "Nothing special. It just seemed likely. I had a hunch . . ."

"You came on damned strong for a guy following a hunch."

He pulled his feet up close to his bottom, got his left elbow on the couch, and peered up at me. "Okay if I get up on this thing?"

"Be my guest."

He grunted, struggled up, settled back, and rubbed his neck. "What's the lady looking for?"

"Clothes for her sister."

"Oh."

"What'd you think she was looking for, jewelry?"

His flat face stayed blank. "Why would I think that?"

"I don't know. Why are you sticking around town?"

"The cops told me not to leave."

"I see. And since you haven't done anything wrong, you figured why not, eh?"

He nodded solemnly.

"Or maybe there's still something you're supposed to do. Maybe a payoff to collect?"

Rita appeared in the hall carrying a folded piece of red silk under her arm.

"Well, it's nice to see you two getting along so nicely," she said. "Can we go now?"

"Find what you were looking for?" asked Podolack politely.

"Uh-huh. Trixie wanted her kimono. I think this is the one she likes best."

"Friday night she wore a green one," said Podolack.

"Well, that wasn't her favorite. Let's go, Carl, if you guys are through chatting."

I decided I wasn't going to get any more out of our friend and started out with Rita, but Podolack called me. I turned.

"I didn't kill Cook," he told me. "That's a fact."

"Sure. You're just a fella passing through."

"No. But I didn't come here to kill him. If I had, I'd be long gone."

"Uh-huh. Whatever, I figure you're as good as long gone already, one way or another."

That puzzled him, as it was supposed to. It even puzzled me a little. I had no idea it'd be prophetic.

Outside we found the tails, looking thoughtful as they stood where the house and city walk met. They waited as we approached and the younger one, who was fair and earnest as a Sunday school teacher, spoke.

"You weren't supposed to enter that house."

"Okay, I won't."

"We have to examine what the lady took out."

"Why?" demanded Rita.

"Orders, ma'am. I'm real sorry, but nothing's to be let out of that house."

I glanced at her, but she only glared at the young man who slowly turned red.

"I'm real sorry," he said, and reached out his hand.

She suddenly smiled, took the silk from under her arm and handed it over. The folded material tumbled open, so brilliant in the sunlight it looked like a giant flame and the young cop accepted it as though expecting a burn.

"Well," he stammered, "well—"

Slowly he took hold with both hands and turned the shimmering silk, examining it inside and out.

"It's not real subtle, is it?" said Rita.

"Uh, no. Thank you, miss, you can have it back if you want. I just had to check it."

Trixie's eyes bugged when she saw the kimono. "Why the hell'd you bring that?"

"I thought you might want to wear it if you decided to sneak out of here some night," said Rita.

Trixie flushed at the sarcasm, started to get mad and instead looked hurt. Rita touched her apologetically and they sat beside each other on the cot.

"There was no necklace," said Rita. "I searched through clothes, shoes, boxes, and lint. Went over the bed, bureaus, and under the carpet in both bedrooms and even checked out the bathroom, including the tank. Trixie, honey, are you *sure* you didn't do something with it?"

Trixie's body jerked, she glared at her sister for a second and then seemed to deflate. "You think I'd lie to you?"

Rita smiled gently, took her hand and squeezed it.

I could see we were heading for a weepy scene and spoke up quick to head it off. "Who'd Bernie say was supposed to get the necklace?"

Trixie looked up. Her eyes were watery, about to leak. "Judge Torkelson. The Norsky saint."

"Hell, he's an old widower."

"Of course. You think an old fool like that'd buy an emerald necklace for his wife?"

"My God, he's too old for—"

"He's not too old to dream."

While I was thinking that over Trixie stood up, took the silk kimono and spread it open. It didn't blaze as brightly as it had in the sun, but it was still enough to warm the room a bit.

"Bernard loved this," she said mournfully. "Gave it to me on my last birthday."

Rita, remembering Bernie's weakness for the riding crop, couldn't resist. "It probably reminded him of blood."

Trixie froze, then turned to glare at her sister. I moved between them and suggested we'd been around long enough, we'd see her the next day. Trixie was too mad to talk, which I thought was lucky at the moment, and out we went.

Ike was sitting on the bench in the hall, smoking his usual stogie and glowering. When I greeted him he only grunted.

Outside the police station Rita and I stopped and squinted at each other in the glaring sunlight.

"I've got to tell Baker about the necklace business," I said.

"Why?"

"He's the only one who can find out some things I've got to know. The necklace business is information I can swap."

"For what?"

"The record on Podolack, background on this Judge Torkelson."

"Why's Podolack so important?"

"Hell, I don't know that he is. But, damn it, he came here for some reason that had nothing to do with looking for work in construction. Why'd Trixie dress special that night? Did Bernie know Podolack'd be there?"

"You figure it out, you're supposed to be the detective or what am I paying you for?"

"I'm trying, but the more I work at it the better punching cows looks."

"Don't be silly. Okay, go back and see the man. If he doesn't stick you in the pokey, come around and see me tonight."

"You can bet on it."

Chapter 22

Sergeant Wendtland was at the duty desk and told me Lieutenant Baker was busy so I strolled back and sat on the wooden bench beside Ike. He gave me a look I couldn't read, somewhere between hostile and grateful, if you can picture it.

"What's going on?" I asked.

He jerked his head toward Baker's door. "He's got Adair back there."

"Oh?"

"Sent two bulls to bring her down. He could've phoned, you know, but he sends these guys to scare her and so everybody on the block sees her being dragged to the station."

"Dragged? What'd she do, resist?"

"Nah. You know what I mean—the way it looks . . ."

"How long's she been in there?"

"Over half an hour. That's a hell of a while for

three big bastards to bully one little girl in a room with the door closed."

His voice was thin. When I first noticed that I thought it was from rage, then I realized it was fear. His hand shook when he took the cigar from his mouth and coughed.

"Didn't they want to talk with you?" I asked.

"No. They even tried to make me stay at home, the bastards. I wanted to go get a lawyer but Adair wanted me to stay with her and I promised I'd be here."

His voice got huskier as anger took over.

"Is it true you carry a knife on your ankle when you play poker?" I asked.

His head jerked around and he glared at me. "Where the hell'd you hear that?"

"Around."

"It's bullshit. I haven't done it in twenty years."

"But you used to?"

"For a while. After two guys lifted a roll off me when I'd beat 'em square."

"I heard you tote a gun, too."

"Now and again." He wasn't ashamed of the gun.

"When you played poker at Bernie's?"

He snorted. "Hell, no. Why'd I need a gun with those boy scouts?"

"Maybe you figured a guy like Podolack'd show up."

He straightened up and rested his elbows on the bench back.

"That bohunk didn't scare me."

"He try?"

"Guys like that always try. Sat there, giving me the old deep scowl and tough mug. I toughed him back and bluffed him out of calling me when I'd split openers. He doesn't know shit about poker."

191

When Baker's door opened, Ike rose, quick as a kid, and darted toward it. Adair came out followed by a plainclothesman. Ike grabbed Adair who put her head on his shoulder and hugged him.

"We're going home," Ike told the plainclothesman.

"Fine."

Ike, with tears in his eyes, hustled Adair past me. The plainclothesman gave me a cold stare.

"I'm Wilcox," I said. "I want to see the lieutenant."

Baker was standing by his window, staring at the bricks across the alley as I moved inside. He turned casually, adjusted his glasses with one hand, and eased down on the wide windowsill.

"Get anything from the girl?" I asked.

"Maybe. What do you want now?"

"I'd like to make a little swap."

"Yeah, what the hell'd you have to offer me?"

"How well do you know Judge Torkelson?"

"We aren't exactly lodge brothers."

"What's his reputation? Shady, clean?"

"All judges got clean reputations. Especially old ones."

"You know if he's got a girl friend?"

He scowled. "What the hell has Judge Torkelson's sex life got to do with anything?"

"There's a story around that he plans to buy, or already bought, a hot necklace for his lady friend. Bernie sold hot jewelry."

Baker stood, walked over to his chair and sat down.

"Tell me more."

"I don't know much more. Podolack might, though."

Baker rested both elbows on the desk and hunched his broad shoulders. "So you went around to Bernie's place this afternoon and found Podolack waiting out in front?"

"That's right. Came up with sniffles. Did your guys find the necklace?"

Slowly he grinned at me. "Wouldn't you like to know?"

I decided they hadn't. "What I'd really like to know is what you've found out about Podolack."

"One conviction. Assault. Picked up on suspicion in bootlegging hassles and loan-shark enforcing. Nothing real big or bad."

"Any connection with Stuckey?"

"They came from the same town."

We sat awhile, thinking things over. I don't know if it helped him any, but it didn't get me anywhere.

"I guess maybe we should pick him up," said Baker. "Sweat him a little."

"Let me talk to him again first. I'll go over to his place."

He stared at me through his blanking-out lenses for a second, then, to my surprise, said okay.

Podolack's landlady came to the door when I knocked. She was tall, and as gaunt and friendly as an underfed watchdog. A plain brown dress hung from her shoulders to her ankles with no more shape than if it were draped over a wire hanger. Graying hair straggled from a tight bun at the back of her scrawny neck.

"I'm looking for Mr. Podolack," I told her.

"Gone." The tone implied good riddance.

"Permanent?"

She nodded.

"Say where?"

"Nope."

"Paid up?"

193

"That's between him and me."

"You don't expect him back, I don't suppose?"

"Not to stay."

That was confusing and she knew it. I was ornery enough to ignore the obvious next question and asked when he'd first come around.

"Why'd you want to know that?"

"He was playing poker last Friday night at a house where a man got murdered."

"I know that. What's it to you?"

"I'm trying to help the murdered man's wife. She's been accused of doing it. Her sister doesn't believe she did, neither do I. I'm trying to find out what really happened."

"He's a bad man," she said, jerking her chin down.

"Who?"

"Podolack."

"What makes you say that?"

"He smoked in his room. Burned a hole in the sheet and mattress. Told me he didn't smoke. Lied."

"So you threw him out?"

"Didn't know he'd done it till he went today. Smelled smoke. Found the sheet and mattress ruined. What I can't stand is being lied to, barefaced like that."

"When'd you say he moved in?"

"Didn't. But it was Friday morning. The day that fella was murdered."

"What time did he show up?"

"Long about ten-thirty. Said he wanted a quiet room, off the street. I said he had to pay a week in advance. He said he didn't know he'd be around that long. I said it's a dollar and a half a day, paid in advance, or seven a week. He said he'd take the week and paid me with a five dollar bill and two ones. Nice new money. You think he murdered that fella?"

"It's possible."

"He had the eyes for it."

"Oh?"

She jerked her chin again. "Murder in those eyes."

"Did he leave anything in his room?"

"Didn't leave nothing but a ring in the tub."

It was nice to know Podolack was clean, however mean. I thanked her for being so helpful, and she said that was all right, she hoped I caught him.

I made a quick report to Lieutenant Baker and then swung around to Rita's hotel where I caught up with her just as she was getting on the elevator. She listened to my tale of Podolack's betrayal of the landlady without any noticeable enthusiasm and asked what was next.

"I don't know," I said as we got off the elevator and started down the hall. "Maybe Baker'll pick him up."

She handed me her key and I unlocked the door and pushed it open. She took two steps and halted as Mr. Stuckey appeared at the corner beyond the closet wall to our left. Then Chuck, who'd been waiting behind the door, gave it a shove, knocking me off balance, and snatched Rita's wrist with one hand while grabbing for her purse with the other. He was grinning. Her left hand came up, stiff-fingered, hawk-swift, and shot straight into his eyes. He yelled, dropped her wrist and jerked both hands to his face. She promptly swung her purse back-handed into his crotch.

Stuckey, frozen for a second, stared open-mouthed as I jerked Rita back into the hall and slammed the door before Chuck's yell stopped. The next moment we were pounding down the hall,

195

through the stairway door and on down, clattering and puffing.

We slowed to a fast walk in the lobby, and I went to the clerk and told him two guys were in Rita's room and he should call the cops.

He gaped and asked if I were sure.

"Positive. Names are Stuckey and Chuck, the cops know them. Go on, damn it, call!"

"You're really something," I told Rita as I hustled her out the front door. "You make me feel about as dangerous as a declawed tabby."

"I've never liked being grabbed," she said. She didn't sound at all defensive.

"I'm sure glad as hell I started slow with you."

She grinned but looked pale and it gave me some relief. No doubt she could take care of herself, but she didn't gloat over it, and she didn't ask how come we'd run while we were ahead. That would've made me feel awful.

The hot wind blew hair across her face and she held it back as she hiked briskly beside me, blinking against the sun and dust.

"I've seen your two favorite targets on a man," I said. "Have you got a third?"

She tilted her head to look at me. "The ears. You can hurt a guy good by slapping your palms over both ears at once. A fist in the Adam's apple is good if you've only got one hand free, but it's not as easy to reach if his chin's down."

"My God, you've made a whole study of combat."

"It's been handy. What've you learned in all your fights?"

"Never start an argument with your hands in your pockets."

She nodded thoughtfully but wasn't too impressed since she'd probably never had pockets.

* * *

Baker wasn't in so I told our story to Sergeant Wendtland who'd already sent two cops over after getting the hotel clerk's call. He said he was disappointed in me. From all he'd heard I should've brought those two hoods in, one under each arm.

We went back to see what our two playmates had done to Rita's hotel room before we arrived.

They'd been very busy. Rita was mad, but I thought the hotel manager would cry when he took in the slashed mattress, lounge, and easy chair. There was stuffing all over the place and all the drawers had been dumped and clothing was strewn around.

"I just wish I'd hit that gorilla harder," grated Rita as she picked up gowns and kicked aside stuffing.

"You did pretty well."

"We didn't lay a hand on Stuckey." She sounded accusing.

"He wasn't real handy, and he had a gun."

"I didn't see it."

"So why else did he have his hand in his pocket?"

"Maybe he hasn't learned as much about fighting as you have."

The manager fluttered around, telling us nothing like this had *ever* happened in *his* hotel before we showed up. I asked how long it'd take to make the place livable again and he said probably *forever*. He was going to say more, but after looking at me he excused himself and went downstairs. Ten minutes later the elevator operator and a young bellhop came in and nervously told me they'd been ordered to say Mrs. Gate's room couldn't be restored for at least a week and there were no other rooms available.

"She won't have to pay for today," the bellhop told me earnestly, "even though it's past check-out time."

"Why didn't that slimy weasel tell me that himself?" I asked.

"He was scared to," the bellhop said.

"It's all right," said Rita. "I'd rather get out of here."

The young men beamed at her and bowed out.

I shook my head. "What's the etiquette for getting kicked out of a hotel? Do you tip the guys that told you?"

"I don't know, you could write to Emily Post."

"I'm glad you didn't figure it called for a purse to the privates and fingers in the eye. Where do you want to go?"

"Out. Get my suitcases, will you? I've got to pack."

She picked up her stuff, folded it swiftly, and packed each piece as if it had an assigned space.

"You travel a lot?" I asked.

"Now and again. Probably nothing to your record."

That seemed likely. For one thing, she hadn't lived long enough.

A cop was waiting for us downstairs. He wouldn't take our luggage and I got the clerk to agree on storage for a couple of hours.

"You hear what happened?" asked Baker when we came in.

"I thought we were in the middle of what happened," I said.

"We found Podolack."

"Oh. Got him locked up?"

"Didn't have to. He's not going anywhere."

"Ah."

"You don't sound surprised."

"I don't know what to be surprised about."

Baker looked at Rita. "How about you, are you surprised?"

"You're telling us he's dead, is that it?"

"If he's not, the coroner's gonna be damned surprised. He ordered an autopsy."

"How'd it happen?" I asked.

Baker stared at me for a moment. "When's the last time you talked with Podolack?"

"At Bernie's house, while your guys were standing outside."

"You haven't seen him since?"

"No."

"You two had a fight in there, didn't you?"

"Just a little argument."

"Uh-huh. It got so wordy somebody landed on the floor."

"Your guys must've been peeking through the keyhole."

"They heard the crash. What'd you hit him with?"

"A little rabbit punch."

He shook his head. "One of these days somebody's going to catch you coming in and we'll pick you up with a shovel."

"Probably."

"What was the fight about?"

I told him.

He nodded and asked where did I figure he fitted in.

"I'm stumped," I told him. "He doesn't seem to fit in anywhere."

"The way I see it, he's part of the Stuckey-Chuck team. They figured he double-crossed them and stuck his head in the river. Why do you figure those two clowns tried to hit you today?"

"Still looking for the necklace."

He asked for a rundown on the fracas and I laid it out.

199

"My God," he said. "Why'd you drag her out? Why not just turn her loose and let her wipe them out?"

"I knew Stuckey had a gun. I didn't want her body messed up."

"Not to mention your own carcass."

"I'm fond of that too."

He took off his glasses and set them on the desk. I could see deep pad marks in his hide where the nose and eyes nearly met. They made him look strangely vulnerable.

"The hotel's thrown Rita out," I said. "I'm going to put her up at the Wilcox Hotel in Corden, okay?"

"We got other hotels here," he said, reaching for his glasses.

"Yeah, but those two guys can't move around in Corden without being as obvious as turds on a butcher block."

"So they'll be obvious. Who's gonna stop them?"

"Joey Paxton's a good cop."

"Maybe. But he's alone. You want to get him killed?"

"I'll have Rita around."

"Oh, well, with her around, what more could a man need?"

"I've been thinking about Podolack."

"Yeah, explain him to me."

"I think he's a new supplier. Old Bernie wasn't too happy with Stuckey and Chuck, he wanted another connection for classier stuff that'd bring faster money."

"Sure." Baker nodded. "There must be all kinds of markets for classy jewels in this town. Probably could sell minks in Corden, too."

I admitted that wasn't too likely but reminded him Bernie hadn't been the most brilliant guy in the world and one hot deal would convince him he was on his way to millions. We kicked that around until finally I asked if he'd talked with Judge Torkelson about Podolack.

"I gave it a try," he admitted. "He said he'd never heard of the man."

"I guess that didn't surprise you too much."

He was shaking his head when the telephone rang. He answered, frowned at the voice on the other end, shifted his chair and leaned forward on his elbows. I politely gazed out his window and watched a butterfly flit along the brick wall, lift and suddenly dart from sight. Baker grunted twice, said yessir four times and finally said yes, he understood. He hung up the receiver very carefully and sat with his hands folded on the desk while he stared glumly at me.

"Now what?" I asked.

He leaned back, pulling his hands off the desk. "You planning to talk with the judge?" he asked too casually.

"Will it get me arrested?"

"It might."

"What kind of a charge?"

"I don't know, but if he brings it, it'll be a dandy."

"You're telling me to lay off."

"Don't be dumb. I'm daring you to try him. If you've got the guts, come back and let me know what you learned, and who knows, maybe I can help you out."

I looked at him for a while, then stood up. "Will you have somebody keep an eye on Rita while I'm at it?"

He grinned. "I've got a whole police force that'd love to keep both eyes on this young lady. Be tactful with the judge, eh?"

Chapter 23

The judge lived in a three-story house with a round tower on the right front, a wide porch reached by four steps that faced the street corner and gingerbread wood trim dripping like icicles all across the eaves. The lawn was a quarter of a mile deep and sloped gently down to the sidewalk. There was a matching shed out back that once sheltered the outdoor toilet, but it had been a good many years since anyone had ventured out there for relief since the indoor plumbing was as splendid, according to reports, as any in the county. I wouldn't know first-hand, never having been invited for tea.

Nothing was doing out front, so I drove around the south side and there was the judge busy weeding with help from a young man. I pulled over, parked and strolled across the watered lawn toward them. The young man looked up, saw me and spoke to the judge who rose from his knees and squinted my way.

"Nice weather for weeds," I observed when I was within a couple yards of him.

"Ideal," he admitted with a smile not quite as warm as the sun but cordial enough. He had a red tan, white hair, blue eyes, and excellent store teeth. I guessed him at sixty or so. His bare arms were brown and covered with fine gray hairs. He stood straight with squared shoulders.

"My name's Wilcox."

His tufted eyebrows raised. "Wilcox? That sounds familiar."

"My folks own the Wilcox Hotel in Corden, come to Aquatown every week and meet with the Old Timers Club. They're pretty well-known."

"I think they're better known for their offspring."

"Well . . ."

"There's a daughter, I believe, used to be a town belle as I recall. Broke a dozen hearts when she married a fellow and moved out of the state."

"Yeah, that's my sister, Ruth."

"Yes. Model daughter. And the son, he was something else. Carl. Right?"

"You don't miss a bet, Judge."

His smile warmed. "It's amazing what anomalies one set of parents can produce, isn't it?"

"Just what Ma says. Not exactly those words, of course."

"So what'd you want to talk with me about?"

"Well, it's kind of touchy," I said, glancing at the sun-bleached young man.

"Floyd," said the judge, "why don't you just trot up to the house and get us some iced tea?"

The boy nodded, put down his hoe and walked toward the house, mopping his forehead with a red bandanna.

"Fine boy," said the judge, then peered at me with a kindly smile. "You in some kind of trouble?"

"Not the usual kind, no. I'm working for a lady whose sister is accused of killing her husband."

"Ah, yes, the Cook affair. So what do you want from me?"

"Well, there are some strange types involved in all this. . . ."

"From what I've heard of Cook, I don't doubt it."

"Yeah, and there've been some stories spread around I've got to check on, no matter how screwy they sound."

"I see. And I bet that pretty soon you're going to get to the point of all this, right?"

"One story says you were going to buy a necklace from Bernie. A very expensive one."

"Is that right? Did they say what I planned to do with it?"

"It's supposed to be for a lady friend."

"Well"—he beamed—"that's a comfort. I was afraid they'd told you I wanted to wear it myself. Okay, let me ask a question. Now that you've seen me, do you think I might have a lady friend I'd buy stolen jewelry for?"

"I'm not too sure."

His grin broadened. "You don't think I'm too old for a lady friend?"

"No, not at all."

"I could be an old fool, right?"

"Over the right kind of woman, I'd guess so."

He chuckled. "You're just about what I'd expect from what I've heard. Did you actually ride a jackass backwards to a funeral?"

"I'm afraid so."

"And climbed a watertower to paint the light on top red?"

"I guess you've heard them all."

"Oh, yes, I may be an old fool, but I still remember everything. Like I remember that smart policemen now and then use certain criminal types to get information." He beamed at me. "You haven't, by any chance, been talking with Lieutenant Baker?"

"Yeah, I've talked with him a lot. In this case and one before. But I work for Rita, not the lieutenant. All I'm after is information that'll help Trixie beat the rap."

"Of course. And you're convinced she didn't kill her husband, right?"

"Rita is, and she knows her sister better than anyone else could."

"That doesn't mean she knows the woman well enough to say whether she'd kill under the right circumstances. And from what I hear, the circumstances were perfect for murder."

"Judge, did you ever deal with Bernie?"

"Never saw the man."

"How about a man named Podolack?"

"Name doesn't mean a thing."

"Husky guy, early thirties, looks like a hod carrier and claims he was. Did some collection work for loan sharks in Chicago. He was at the poker game in Cook's house the night Cook died."

The judge looked over my shoulder and said, "Ah, here comes our iced tea."

Floyd, with the sun-bleached hair, brought a tray with a pitcher and three ice-filled glasses. The judge tilted his head and Floyd walked east of the garden and placed the tray on a small picnic table under a box elder. I followed the judge and sat down across from him. Floyd sat beside me. The judge gazed at his young helper with a grandfatherly expression.

"You must beware of Mr. Wilcox," he said. "He is a

man with a colorful and checkered past. He drinks, brawls, chases women—often catches them, I hear—commits practical jokes, paints signs and houses, was once a rustler, and is often on the bum. Avoid all contact or he'll corrupt you beyond redemption."

Floyd gave me an apologetic smile. I guessed he was about sixteen.

The judge shook his head ruefully. "You probably couldn't corrupt him. Floyd already knows about my being involved with a lady half my age who is excessively attractive and should turn his head completely."

"Who is she?" I asked him.

"I'm not going to tell you. I know your reputation too well; I'll take no chances on your meeting her."

"You did arrange to buy a necklace for her, didn't you?"

"I was made an offer. A very attractive one."

"By Bernie?"

"His emissary."

"Who was he?"

He sipped his iced tea, put down the tinkling glass and smiled. "You assume it was a man."

"Was that a mistake?"

"Now you'll suspect so," he said happily.

"That's right. I figured it was probably Podolack."

"If you were going to offer to sell me something, would you send a man who looked like a hoodlum?"

"Good point," I granted.

"I shouldn't have to do your work for you, you know."

"That's right, the pay's not good enough. So maybe you'd be more receptive to a young lady—maybe one named Adair?"

"I'm always receptive to young ladies. Don't get many chances."

"This one was in love with Bernie. She wore stuff he was selling."

"I assume she's pretty?"

"How'd she strike you?"

"Never struck me at all. Never heard of her."

He was having a wonderful time and I might have enjoyed it more if I hadn't felt it was all at my expense. I drank some iced tea and asked if he didn't have any sugar.

"Floyd," said the judge, "get Mr. Wilcox some sugar."

The boy went off.

"He's a little simple," said the judge. "Not an idiot, just simple. No sense of humor. Almost a perfect servant, very careful, respectful, and obedient. No foolish ambitions or mean impulses. Precisely what God had in mind when he made Adam, I suspect, but he didn't quite pull it off. Do you begin to get the feeling you're not getting anywhere, Mr. Wilcox?"

"Uh-huh."

He rested his folded arms on the table and looked thoughtful.

"I had a telephone call a while back. From a person I've known rather slightly over the years. This person knew the young lady who interests me and after a rather protracted conversation that seemed as pointless as what you and I have been covering, he remarked that the lady in question was fond of jewelry and he knew someone who could make something rather special available to me at a remarkably low cost."

"Just like that?"

"Yes. It struck me as most strange, I'll admit. I

tried to think what the point might be and blackmail came to mind. I was intrigued."

"You wanted to be blackmailed?"

"Well, not if it involved bribery or something equally unsavory—but over my involvement with a young lady? That'd be intriguing."

"I wish your line of guff didn't keep swinging from matter to malarkey, Judge. I can't decide when to believe you."

"Sometimes I almost confuse myself."

"Wasn't it more like you made the telephone call that started this business with the necklace?"

"Absolutely not. I wouldn't have known who to call. Never knew anything but a nickname for the party."

"You called the party 'he' twice, Judge, so you've shot that piece of confusion."

"Ah, but did I make the slip deliberately?"

"I doubt it."

Floyd came back carrying a blue glass sugar bowl. He placed it before me and sat down again. The spoon in the bowl was a silver souvenir piece covered with tiny bas-relief scenes including a river with a paddle wheeler, and a farmer plowing behind a horse. I turned the spoon and examined the back, which was covered with Indian relics—a teepee, canoe, war club, tomahawk, and peace pipe.

"Lovely piece, eh?" said the judge as I measured out sugar. "Bought it for my wife forty years ago."

"You buy her any jewelry?"

"A gold wedding band. Not even a big one. Didn't have money in those days. Probably wouldn't have spent it on her if I'd had it then. Martha wasn't a flashy woman, liked things for the kitchen and house. Very practical most ways—liked fancy dishes, the serving kinds, you know? Big bowls with painted flowers, little bowls on ball legs and fine silver, good glassware. We bought a lot of that stuff the year before she died. A fine woman."

After the last statement he sat quietly for a moment, thinking about it.

"Dull as dishwater, actually." He looked sad.

Floyd sipped the iced tea and gazed at the garden. The judge stirred, looked at the boy and suggested he go back to weeding when he finished his tea. The boy nodded, took another sip and left us, giving me a polite nod as he turned.

"I guess the lady you picked the necklace for is a bit different," I said.

"Perfect opposite." He said that with satisfaction and suddenly grinned at me. "You understand that, don't you?"

"Yeah, I do."

"Like you're just the opposite of any people I ever socialized with when I was young and ambitious. In those days, I wouldn't have let a man like you on my property. Would've turned the dogs loose—if I'd had any dogs."

"I'd guess Trixie's like your new lady," I said.

"Trixie? Oh, yes, the murdered man's widow. I understand she's a bit flamboyant. I assume you know her well?"

"Not that well."

"What about the sister," he said. "Do you know her better?"

"I haven't known her as long."

"A careful answer. You sound like a man in court. You take both of these ladies seriously, don't you?"

I nodded.

"You think it'd really make any difference if I told you all I know?"

"I won't know until you tell me."

His face turned solemn and he leaned over the picnic table. "I wouldn't want my lady's name to come up in relation to any of this business."

"I don't know her name and I won't ask again."

He nodded thoughtfully. "All right. You want the liaison person. The lady put me in touch with him. He called me because she called him and I put her up to it, rather indirectly. I told her I wanted to buy something extravagant—an investment piece, you might say. We discussed it very thoroughly. My lady's a good businesswoman, very intelligent, thoughtful, and greedy in a healthy way. She said I'd spend too much in a jewelry store for what I'd get. I'd heard about Bernard Cook's little business with his city friends and suggested him as the one to deal with, but she said he was a tinhorn, too indiscreet and unreliable."

"So you didn't really think somebody was setting you up for blackmail when you got the call?"

He grinned and pulled back a little. "You don't miss a thing, do you? You'd make quite a court reporter. Now don't interrupt, all right? I told my lady, why don't you just buy a house and some property, and she said she already had a house and those things could always burn down and aren't portable. The necklace, she said, would be like money in the bank only much more beautiful."

"I suppose this guy she steered you to has a name?"

"Oh, yes, I suspect you know it."

I suggested the name I had in mind.

"Well," he said respectfully, "perhaps you are a detective after all. Just remember, my lady's name doesn't come up."

"Don't worry."

"I won't back you up on a thing I've said, you know. Not one thing."

"I never thought you would. So long, Judge."

"Give my regards to Lieutenant Baker," he said, and grinned.

Chapter 24

Back at the station I found Rita in the hall, talking with Lieutenant Baker. She looked mad and I figured Baker had been giving her trouble, but it turned out she was sore at Trixie.

"She wants a new lawyer," said Rita, "and she thinks you're useless."

"She's not too dumb," said Baker, grinning at me.

"What do you think?" I asked her.

"I think she's an idiot, but maybe right. What'd you get from the judge?"

I said I wasn't sure and suggested we go into the lieutenant's office. He waved us in, Rita took the chair, I parked on the corner of the desk, and Baker took the throne.

"The judge admitted he made a deal to buy a necklace for his lady friend. You know who she is?"

"Bitsy Bach. A widow across the alley from his place."

"*Bitsy?*"

"Uh-huh. Probably for Elizabeth. Real small woman with the kind of face you see on cameo brooches, you know?"

"How long's she been a widow?"

"Since about a year ago when her husband had an accident in the cities. Fell down a hotel stairway."

"Didn't the place have an elevator?"

"Uh-huh. He was afraid of them. Always took stairs. The bellhops confirmed that, in case you're planning to slander the judge."

"Have you talked with her?"

Baker smiled a little grimly. "She told me to ask the judge any questions I might have."

We thought that over a few seconds before Rita hitched around and asked did I intend to try the lady? I looked at Baker.

"Why not? You seem to have done fine with the judge. You'd probably be even better with the woman."

"I'll come along," said Rita.

I had a feeling that wouldn't help a lot and looked to Baker for help but he only grinned and shook his head. "It's your problem, pal."

"Anyway," said Rita, "it's time for dinner. We'll eat and talk it over and then see this woman."

We went to Fino's, and Rita went through her steak even faster than usual and watched me impatiently as I finished my hamburger. She was raring to go.

"I think you're in a hurry to get out of South Dakota," I said.

"Why'd you think that? Just because the towns are dull and the weather's awful. . . ."

"You just need another round with Chuck."

"I'm bored with him too."

213

"Well, cheer up, I don't think it'll be long before you can go home."

She was lifting her coffee cup when I spoke and she stopped it in mid-air to narrow her eyes at me. "The judge told you something?"

"Uh-huh."

"So how long are you going to be cute before you tell me?"

"Tiny Sorenson was the go-between on the necklace."

She took a drink from the cup, put it back in the saucer and shook her head. "I don't believe it. He's been in love with Trixie for years."

"That's one of the reasons it makes sense. You know what they say about love and hate—next-door neighbors. And remember, Tiny was a strong man with the carnival before he became a barker. He's sloppy now, but he's no marshmallow like you might think."

"So where does Podolack come in?"

"I think Tiny got the necklace through him. He probably got knocked off because Stucky figured he was unfair competition."

She frowned and told me I wasn't making sense. I didn't argue because she was mostly right and since my appetite had died before the hamburger was gone I folded up my napkin and we left.

We approached the widow's house a little after seven. It stood on a flat lot with a parched lawn and had the usual two floors and high attic typical of the neighborhood. Its paint was powdery on the white clapboard walls, the wide porch had fresh-painted screens, and the tall windows overlooking the street gleamed in the late sun, which threw long shadows from the lilac bushes flanking the white sidewalk.

We sashayed up the walk, climbed the three steps,

and I knocked. A young girl appeared in the inner doorway and walked solemnly to the screen. She was about eight, blonde as an actress and neater than fresh-folded laundry.

"Hi," I said. "Is your mother home?"

"She's not my mother, she's my aunt." Her blue eyes took me in at a glance and then studied Rita with interest.

"Would you tell her we'd like to see her?"

"She's already got company."

"Oh. Give her a message, will you? Tell her Carl Wilcox wants to talk to her about a necklace."

That got her attention. "That's a funny message."

"Yeah. See if she laughs."

She turned with dignity, walked to the door and then took off down the hall, skipping.

"Who do you think the guest is?" asked Rita.

"I just hope it's not two guys we know."

Before we could go on about that the widow appeared, all golden hair, delicate features, and perfect skin.

"Yes?" she said in a husky voice.

"Mrs. Bach?"

"That's right. What'd you say to my niece?"

"That I wanted to talk to you about a necklace."

She drew in her breath which expanded her chest nicely and frowned just enough not to cause unsightly wrinkles.

"I guess you'd better come inside," she said, and pushed the screen open. I stepped aside, letting Rita enter first, then moved in and introduced them. They examined each other without sniffing aloud and then she led us inside.

Heavy drapes and drawn blinds kept heat and light from the big parlor so I was feeling my way like a blind man. The widow took my elbow, steered me to an easy chair and apparently helped Rita too because I didn't hear her stumble. It took a few blinks before I could make out the hostess sitting on a couch across from us. There was a dark shape sitting to her right. For half a second I thought it was Chuck before I realized it was too big for him.

"Hello, Carl," said the hulk.

"Hi, Tiny," I answered.

Rita leaned foward. "You're Big Tiny Sorenson?"

"All of me," he admitted.

"They're old carny friends," I explained. "Bitsy was a performer with Trixie—right?"

"I was a dancer, yes."

I looked at the cameo face under the haloing hair and tried to imagine her on a girlie show stage. It seemed as unnatural as a doe grazing with oxen.

As my eyes adjusted to the dim light I saw the room was furnished like Ma's parlor only with more dough than she'd ever thought was moral. The chairs and couch had antimacassars, the marble-topped side tables were draped in red plush with long gold tassels. The carpet was thick and redder than a harlot's mouth. All the furniture squatted on wooden feet that turned out duck fashion. I could imagine it settling to the floor like a bunch of crocodiles when the room was deserted for the night.

"You two been close ever since the carny days?" I asked.

"Not really," she said. "We seldom see each other."

"So what gives today?"

She smiled serenely. "The judge would call it serendipity."

"I'll bet he would, but what would he mean?"

The smile widened, showing dimples and small white teeth. "Sort of like good luck."

"Is he delivering the necklace?" asked Rita who was not given to sneaking up on a key question.

Bitsy looked at her as if she'd spoken in Chinese.

Rita, annoyed, leaned forward, dark and intense as she faced Tiny. "You thought of the necklace for this woman, didn't you? Or did she suggest it herself? And then you arranged things with Podolack and he came here with the necklace, but something went wrong."

Tiny's face sagged like an old pillow propped against a headboard. "Everything went wrong."

"Was Podolack supposed to kill Bernie?" I asked.

"Of course not. All he was supposed to do was deliver the necklace to the judge when the money was available. The people in Chicago had been supplying Bernie, but since Bitsy didn't trust him, they slipped Podolack in so's it'd seem Bernie wasn't involved. *I* didn't have any connections except Bernie so when I explained to him what was up he thought it was all very funny. I didn't know he was already in trouble with the Chicago men. So what happened was, Podolack came and insisted I take him to Bernie's poker party and Bernie knew who he was and started teasing him with Trixie and as usual he went too far. When we all left, Podolack sneaked back, smothered Bernie, and took the necklace. Then he hung around, trying to make a deal with the judge himself, only he wanted a higher price than had been agreed on. The judge said no, and when Chuck and Mr. Stuckey came around, I told them Podolack had the necklace. They looked him up and you know what happened."

For a moment we all sat in the gloom and stared at him.

"Can you prove any of this?" I asked.

"Nobody can. Nobody'll try. Not unless they want to end up in the river."

"What about Trixie?" demanded Rita.

"That's all I think about," said Tiny miserably.

"I'll bet," said Rita, glaring at him.

"So where's the necklace now?" I asked Bitsy. She gave a delicate shrug. "*I* haven't got it."

I looked at Tiny. He stared back at me, a big, sagging hulk with droopy jowls and a chinful of folds halfway to his collarbone. His loosely knotted tie was cockeyed and his starched collar cut into his fat neck. His small eyes watched me warily.

"How come you're so sure Podolack killed Bernie?" I asked.

"How else could he've got the necklace?"

"I don't know he had it."

"Well, of course he did, he couldn't have called to offer me a deal if he hadn't, could he?"

"If he committed murder for it, why didn't he just go back to Chicago where there was a real market?"

"I guess he was afraid the piece was too well-known there."

I shook my head. "Uh-uh. It was you, old friend. You killed Bernie and framed Trixie because you've been nuts about her for years, and that Friday night, watching Bernie offer her to this stranger, you just went over the edge. You snuck back knowing he'd be alone because you waited around and saw Trixie leave. You knew that's the sort of thing she'd do when she got mad enough. You went in, found the necklace, took it, put the pillow over Bernie's face and went home. When Podolack figured out what happened he tried leaning on you and made the mistake of thinking you were a marshmallow. You met by the river and drowned him."

Bitsy laughed as Tiny sadly shook his head.

"You've got a great imagination," Bitsy told me. "Just picture poor old Tiny climbing those stairs at Bernie's, putting a pillow over him and then later wrestling with a young tough by the river and pushing his head under. That's ridiculous."

"He could handle it."

"No," she said in her husky voice as she shook her head. "Tiny's a big, sweet old lump. He can be hurt, but he can't hate and he's simply never taken a chance in his life. If you attacked him, he'd cover his face and turn away, even though he's big and strong enough to crush you."

She turned and patted his thick knee kindly. "It's all right, Tiny, I understand. You're just a completely decent man."

"Let's go," said Rita, getting up.

"Hold on, we're not through yet."

She jerked her dark head but settled down once more.

"Your story's full of holes," I told Tiny. "You said Podolack brought the necklace, then you said he stole it from Bernie after smothering him. Now I know Trixie saw the necklace before Friday night, so it was delivered before then. And from what else I know, Podolack didn't hit town until that morning, so when the hell could he have delivered it? And why the hell would he deliver it at all if he was going to swipe it back?"

Tiny gave a massive shrug. "He could've delivered it that afternoon and then decided at the game that he'd made a mistake. That he wasn't going to get paid. He could've delivered it that night when I wasn't watching and got sore when Bernie didn't pay him for it right away."

I stared at him for a few seconds and he gazed back, calm as a cud-chewing cow.

"What'd you tell him about Bernie when you and Podolack were talking that afternoon?" I asked him.

"Oh, stuff like what a crazy character Bernie is . . ."

"Did you tell him Bernie had a young girl friend?"

"Well, yeah, I guess so. I mentioned how he had her wear jewelry to show to customers—or guys he hoped would be customers."

"What else did you tell him?"

He stuck out his lower lip, shifted his weight so he seemed to sink deeper into the chair and blinked thoughtfully.

"Well, I might've told him Bernie liked Adair better than any of the other girls he'd been messing with. I didn't offer that. He asked if it was that way and I said I guessed it was."

"Ah, so maybe I figured it wrong. You didn't kill Bernie youself, you just set him up."

He was still looking hurt when we left. I noticed that Bitsy was no longer amused; she looked very thoughtful.

Chapter 25

We got a table at Fino's about half a block from the bar which was doing a mild business. The rest of the joint was deserted except for half a dozen couples eyeing each other at scattered tables in the gloom.

Rita sipped a pink lady and stared at the table top.

"Have you made any sense out of all that?" she asked.

"Not enough. Wish to hell I could talk with Podolack again."

"You aren't likely to—and it probably wouldn't help if you could. I think this whole town's been infected by Bernie Cook. Even the visitors lie. What'd you think of the blonde widow?"

"A slick article."

"I'll bet you'd like to have seen her act."

"Not much."

"Why not?"

"No bottom."

"Is that what interests you most in a woman?"

"No. But skinny butts are for men. There's something stingy about them on a woman."

She watched me, thinking I had Bernie's disease but kind of liking what I said because there was nothing stingy about her behind.

I was trying to think of something else she'd like to hear when Gene Healey, the poker-playing super suit salesman came strolling up, carrying a beer. I introduced him to Rita, and he took a chair from the nearest table and sat down, giving her his selling smile.

"You think Trixie killed her husband, don't you?" she said.

The smile vanished as he flashed me a hurt look and began backtracking.

"Well, now, I didn't exactly say that. I mean, I didn't mean to say it. . . . It's just that he treated her so lousy she had a right to. She should've done it long ago—"

He turned red, realizing he'd only got himself in deeper, but she smiled, letting him off and right away he was all smiley again.

"Bernie had it coming, that's all I meant to say. . . ."

I let him gabble a while longer and finally butted in. "You said you came here after the poker game. How long did you hang around?"

"Oh, I just had a quick one and left."

"So you weren't around long enough to see Trixie come in?"

"Huh?"

"Trixie claims she came here, looking for somebody to talk with."

He shook his head. "I don't believe it. Somebody'd have told me."

"Like who?"

"Everybody. Hell, wait a sec—hey, Polly!"

The waitresss came over. She was plump, brown-eyed and dark-haired. Gene asked if she'd seen Trixie last Friday night. She said no.

"Ask if Moe saw her."

"If she'd been around, I'd have seen her."

"Sure you would, but this is important," I said. "Do us a favor and ask the guy, okay?"

"Sure, honey," she said, and walked off.

"If Polly didn't see her, she wasn't here," said Gene. "That girl doesn't miss a thing."

We watched her stop at the bar and talk with both bartenders. Then she stopped two other waitresses and came back.

"She wasn't here. Nobody saw her."

"So where the devil was she?" Rita asked me.

"We won't find out until morning," I said.

Polly drifted back when we were about through with our drinks, but instead of asking did we want another round she told me there was a call on the public phone for Carl Wilcox. I gawked at Rita who stared back.

"Guess who?" she said.

It was Stuckey.

"You still want to collect four-fifty?" he asked.

"The ante's gone up to five since your last visit."

"Okay, I can understand that. But nobody got hurt and it didn't cost you. You don't blame us for trying, do you?"

"Of course not. And you can't blame me for thinking you're a double-crossing bastard, right?"

That hurt his feelings. I could tell because he didn't laugh.

"Look, friend," he said after a few seconds, "I'm going to square with you. The way things are, Chuck and I need that stuff—"

"Don't bullshit me. It's nothing big and we both know it. You want the necklace. I haven't got it. Whoever knocked off Bernie took it, and I don't know who that was. It wasn't Podolack or you wouldn't be calling me. Now I think I've got a lead, but I won't know for sure before tomorrow."

I listened to the telephone hum for a while.

"Wilcox, how'd you like to make a quick grand?"

"I don't kill people."

"You don't have to. Tip us off on who did it before you tell the cops. That's all. We'll take it from there."

"I told you, I won't know till tomorrow."

"By when?"

"No idea."

I listened to the hum a while more.

"Okay," he said. "Tomorrow be in Fino's again. I'll call. A friend of mine'll hand over the grand when you give me the name. If it checks out, you get another grand. If it doesn't, we'll get you. We wouldn't miss a third time."

I was tempted to tell him it was wonderful how generous a hood could be when he didn't intend to deliver, but I said okay, figuring I could waltz too, and we both hung up.

Chapter 26

It was nearly two
A.M. when we left Fino's, and Rita nixed the notion
of driving to Corden for bargain rates at the Wilcox
Hotel. I spotted our police tail when we started
down the street and waved at him. He didn't wave
back.

We hit three hotels before one accepted us. The
clerks all assumed we were tramps and that made
Rita mad so we wound up actually using the twin
beds we got.

She was even grumpier in the morning. I wouldn't
have minded so much if she hadn't managed to look
sexier than hell despite tangled hair and a bare face.
When I tried to cozy up she told me to go play with
myself.

"You're all alike," she said as she pulled on her
stockings. "All you want is sex, sex, sex."

"Oh, I enjoy a meal now and again."

"And booze."

"True."

"Have you thought of what you're going to do today?"

"How about we have a good breakfast, come back up here and get our money's worth out of the room?"

She gave me a squelching look, which I'd expected and didn't mourn.

"Okay," I said. "I want to talk with Trixie alone."

She'd just pulled her dress on over her head and stopped smoothing it down to give me a long look. "Why alone?"

"I'm going to lay things on the line and I don't want her to have any moral support standing by."

"You're going to bully her."

"Damn right."

"It won't work," she said, and went over to the bureau to start brushing her tangled hair.

"I'll give it a shot. You stay in sight of the cop Baker assigned, okay? Stuckey and Chuck are still around and they're not likely to be in any better mood than you are."

"I can take care of myself."

"Yeah, don't I know it."

She bought a newspaper in the lobby and read while we ate breakfast. Something in the Andy Gump strip make her smile, but nothing I said did.

Well, what the hell, easy come, easy go.

"I'm going over to the station."

She nodded, then lowered the paper and smiled at me. I decided it wasn't really so easy go after all.

"Okay, Sherlock. I'm going to do some shopping, but I'll be back in the hotel by noon. Good luck."

Trixie greeted me glumly and while I figured that was a good sign for my plans, it made me feel lousy about tearing into her.

"They can't ever get an egg to me hot," she

complained. "I haven't had a decent breakfast in a week."

"If you don't start telling the goddamned truth," I said, "you probably won't get to even eat cold ones much longer."

Her mouth sagged as though I'd slapped her, but almost at once she pushed her hands into the neatly madeup cot and straightened to glare at me.

"What kind of talk's that?"

"You lied about Friday night. You never went to Fino's."

"Who says?"

"Every goddamned body that was there. Gene Healey, the waitresses, the bartenders—not one of them says you showed. You think the cops haven't checked that? What the hell do you figure you're going to get by on, a short skirt and crossed legs? They get women on juries too, you know. Most old ladies that hate cute tricks with blonde hair and big tits even when they don't tie their men down and beat them bloody—"

"I never bloodied him!"

"No, you only killed him!"

"You son-of-a-bitch! Get out of here! You're getting paid to help me and all you want to do is bury me!"

"Okay," I said, lowering my voice. "Calm down and listen. You got enough sense to do that?"

"I don't have to listen," she said, but her voice lowered too.

"You do if you don't want to get nailed for murder."

She crumpled like paper crushed in a fist and began to cry.

"You found the necklace, didn't you?"

She nodded.

"You figured it was for Adair, didn't you?"

She sobbed and nodded again.

"So you took it, left Bernie tied to the bed and went to see Ike, right?"

She reached inside her dress top, pulled out a dinky handkerchief, blew her nose and straightened up a bit as she wiped her eyes. After gulping a couple times she whispered, "Yes, how'd you know?"

"Because he'd get mad and he was the only guy you knew tough enough to do something about it."

She stayed bent over, her shoulders hunched and her face hidden by the yellow hair. Then she began talking in a husky subdued voice.

"It's all so awful. So *embarrassing*. And it was all Bernie's fault. I'd never have done anything with anybody like Ike if Bernie hadn't been fooling around all the time. He had this waitress at Fino's he went to bed with afternoons. I knew something was going on because he was so tired nights, you know? God! The humiliation! And one Friday night Bernie pooped out early and Ike stayed late after the other poker players left and we got talking and he was understanding and gentle. You probably can't imagine it, but he can be sweet. At least he was then. So we had a, you know, little affair for a while. It wasn't long before I came to my senses; after all, he was awfully old for me. He was like a father."

"Uh-huh."

She fiddled with her handkerchief, trying to find a dry spot, gave it up, dropped it on the bunk and asked if I'd hand her purse over. I found it on a shelf near the door and put it on her knees. She dug out a fresh hanky, did some mopping up, found her compact and tried to repair the damage. It helped a little. She took a deep breath, arched her back and looked me in the eye.

"I suppose you think I'm really terrible. I guess you know more about me than anybody I've ever met."

"I'm trying."

She gave a snort of laughter, pushed her hands into the cot beside her hips, and tilted her head back. "Well, what the hell. It makes no never mind now, does it?"

"So you gave Ike the necklace?"

"You damned betcha. And I told him Bernie planned to give it to Adair. You know what he did? Dear sweet old Ike? He told me I was an idiot. Oh, he'd told me that before so it didn't come as any shock. He said if the necklace was worth anything it'd be Bernie's ticket out of South Dakota, and when he went, he'd take Adair and leave me flat. He said Bernie didn't have to give Adair a fortune to sleep with her, he'd got her with dime store stuff and a line of crap."

"Then what?"

She turned away and stared into space. "He asked did Bernie know where I was. I said I didn't know or care. He gave me that mean grin and said, 'You think you'll fix him by sleeping with his girl-friend's old man, huh? You think he doesn't already know we messed around?' I said I didn't see how he could know unless Ike had told him and he laughed and said Bernie knew I'd slept with everybody so why'd one more matter? Well, that wasn't so and he knew it and he made me so damned mad we had a real row and then somehow we wound up in bed together only nothing really happened except he turned gentle like the first night I told you about. I guess he was finally too old to do anything else and I felt sorry for him and was real nice back and for a while there everything was real sweet. And then I fell asleep."

"Do you know if he got up and went out?"

"I wouldn't know, Carl, honest. When I go to sleep after all that kind of upset, I just die a little, you know? I mean, you could haul me out of bed and bounce me on the floor and I'd just snooze on."

"Did you tell him you left Bernie tied?"

Her eyes avoided me again. "I suppose so."

"Suppose hell, you told him, didn't you?"

She went back into a slouch and her voice dropped lower. "Yeah. I told him. I knew it'd make him laugh. He patted me and said I was a hell of a women. I was glad I told him then."

"How'd you manage to get up and go home before the cop showed up?"

"Ike woke me at about five."

"I thought you couldn't wake."

"He put his hand over my mouth and nose so I couldn't breathe. If you're not already dead, that wakes you in a hurry."

"So you went home."

"Uh-huh. He didn't want Adair to know about me—I had to tiptoe out. I walked all the way home. It wasn't very light, but there were birds making a racket and it was cold. Right in the middle of summer it seemed colder than winter. I was goose bumps all over and so sleepy I staggered, and I was afraid."

"Of what?"

"Oh, God, everything. I knew things were going to be awful. I never dreamed it'd be what did happen, but I knew Bernie and me were through and everything'd be different, and I wasn't a kid anymore and I'd have tough times. . . ."

"You notice anything strange when you went into the house?"

"I was too shot to notice a body if there'd been one

on the stairs. I sure as hell wasn't going to go untie Bernie so he could pound me. I went straight to the guest room and flopped, and that's where I was when the cop started beating on the door."

"You left the necklace with Ike?"

"Uh-huh. I knew that'd end things with Bernie and me, and when I handed it to Ike that's what I wanted to happen. But then, when I flopped on the bed, I was already figuring I'd talk Ike into giving it back."

She broke off and began to bawl.

I'd been standing since I'd entered the room and it was getting tiresome so I sat down beside her and pretty soon she was leaning against me and I had my arm around her.

"Were you really going to take the rap for Ike?"

"I didn't want anybody to know what I'd done."

"What worried you the most? People knowing you'd gone out to get laid, stealing the necklace, or siccing Ike on Bernie when he was helpless?"

I thought that'd jar her out of bawling and into another mad, but it didn't work. She just bawled harder.

"I didn't want him killed," she choked. "I was mad and wanted to spite him, but I never wanted him dead forever. I loved him."

Nobody wants anything to be final. I stood, walked to the door and turned to look at her. She let herself down on the cot and lay there like a kid with both hands over her face. This time the tears were real.

"I'll send Rita to see you," I said. "Okay?"

She nodded.

"If you tell Baker what really happened, that Ike did it, things might not work out too bad for you."

She stopped sobbing, took her hands from her red face and lifted her head.

"What do you mean?"

"Well, hell, Ike had his own reasons for killing Bernie. So you gave him the setup—if you turn state's evidence, they give you credit, you know."

She sat up slowly. "You mean, I could make a deal?"

"Yeah. Just forget about all of the embarrassment crap and try leveling for a change. I'll send Rita, and you can talk all of this out and with a little luck maybe we can get you loose before too long. Right now, don't say anything to Baker or anybody else around here, okay?"

She smiled doubtfully, then with more confidence. "I knew you'd help me, Carl. I always had faith in you."

"Uh-huh," I said, and left.

Chapter 27

I found Rita back in the hotel room with a new hat and new shoes she called pumps. They had transformed her mood, if not her looks, and miraculously made me look better. They must have because she gave me a hug and a kiss. It wasn't a total miracle though; she wasn't ready to climb in bed.

It took a few minutes to get that sorted out, and then I remembered that Trixie was in great distress and needed the comforts of her sister toot sweet.

She scowled when I told her that. "What'd you do to her?"

"Got her to talk."

"I don't think I want to know how."

"Okay."

She went to the bureau and examined her face for a moment in the mirror, then looked at my reflection. "What'd you find out? Give me the high spots."

So I high-spotted her. She sat down on the bed and clouded up but kept from raining. Finally she took a deep breath, got up, gave me a firm, not quite motherly kiss, and said okay, she'd go offer aid and comfort.

"What're you going to do?" she asked.

"Go see Ike."

"Don't keep your hands in your pockets."

"Right."

Adair came to the door in a robe and slippers. She didn't look alert or cheerful, not to mention friendly.

"What do you want?"

"Where's Ike?"

"Out peddling stuff. He's a salesman, you know?"

"Any notion where he might be?"

"Not the foggiest," she said, and closed the door.

I went down the walk, thinking they don't teach manners like they used to and climbed back in the car before getting a dandy inspiration. It sent me to the judge's house.

The judge's simple assistant, Floyd, was out in the garden alone. I strolled across the drying grass and stopped near the young tomato plants. Floyd looked up and gave me his bland smile.

"Is the judge inside?" I asked.

"No, sir."

"Know where I could find him?"

"He told me not to worry, he'd be back by afternoon."

"When did he leave?"

"I'm not supposed to say."

"It was last night, huh?"

He nodded, not sure whether that was allowed, then decided it was and said, "Yes, sir."

"Did he leave the house alone?"

"Yes, sir."

234

I smiled at him and he smiled back, then looked own at his hoe. The breeze rustled his strawish air. He pushed it off his forehead and looked at me gain.

"Did a couple fellows come around to see him esterday?" I asked him. "A tall man with a sad face nd a short, tubby-looking guy?"

He thought a moment, then shook his head.

I thanked him, went back to my car, drove around he block past Bitsy's house and saw no signs of life. went around the corner, parked under an elm, got ut and strolled slowly down the alley. The husks of ead lilac blossoms rustled softly in the breeze as I valked along the dusty way between the tall bushes. here was a wooden fence along the back of Bitsy's ouse with a latch-string gate. I pulled the string, ushed and moved in, making the rusty hinges queak.

On my left was a shed which I guessed had once een a small stable. Its shingled roof sagged and the vhite paint was so old the wood showed through. he wide lawn was full of dandelions and plantain; he grass had burned brown in the summer sun. It runched under my feet as I approached the house. ust before I stepped up on the stoop I thought I eard voices inside, but by the time I lifted my hand o knock, they stopped. I rapped gently while trying o peer through the screen.

Bitsy appeared.

"Well," she said, giving me her cameo smile, "if it sn't the South Dakota Sherlock."

"Is the judge here?" I asked.

"I'll bet you deduced that."

"No, I just figured it out."

She laughed, opened the door and let me into a arge kitchen with white cabinets that didn't reach the ceiling and a breakfast alcove with a booth where Ike and the judge sat across from each other. The judge was sipping coffee and gave me a twinkly onceover. Ike looked baleful. I wondered if he had his knife on his leg and a gun in his pocket. From his expression, if he did, I was in trouble.

"You're taking in a lot of tramps this morning," told Bitsy.

"All heart, that's me. Want some coffee?"

"Why not?"

"With cream and sugar?"

"He probably wants it with ham and eggs," said the judge.

"With," I said.

I sat next to the judge, took my fixings from my shirt pocket and started building a smoke. Bitsy poured coffee all around, put the pot back on the stove, and perched across from me.

"So what's new?" she asked.

"There's been another killing."

I lit my cigarette and watched Ike. He was either genuinely surprised or a damned good actor. His mouth dropped, then snapped shut.

"Who?" asked Bitsy, looking appropriately solemn.

"Podolack. Guy from Chicago who dropped in on Bernie's last poker session."

Ike lifted his cup, took a sip and licked his lip. They all watched me, waiting.

"It's too bad," I said. "He made a dandy suspect. Now it seems to be narrowing down to Tiny. He's big enough, strong enough. Only I can't figure a really good motive since I know the victim didn't have the necklace."

I smiled at Ike. He looked at his coffee cup, picked it up and drank again. I'd like to have noticed his and was shaky, but it wasn't. When he looked up his gaze was defiant.

"I know where Trixie went Friday night," I told him.

"Oh?"

"She's not going to take the rap for you, Ike. You must've known that all along."

"So she brought me the necklace. So what? She did that after putting the pillow on him. What's anybody gonna pin on me? Adultery?"

"How about receiving stolen goods?"

"She handed it over, a gift. I took it, just to keep it in the family, you might say. They won't put me away for that."

I looked at Bitsy. She smiled, relaxed and regal as a Siamese cat with her blue eyes taking everything in. Her fine mouth turned up at the corners. She looked innocent as a child watching a puppet show.

"Does the necklace still seem like a good investment to you?" I asked.

She smiled. "I'm afraid I don't know what you're talking about."

I looked at the judge. He was still twinkly and tolerant.

"You just don't seem to be getting anywhere at all, Wilcox," he said.

"How about you, Judge? Are you getting anywhere?"

"I never had any distant destination. I like it here and I'm still well ensconced."

"And you're willing to let Trixie take the rap?"

"I've always believed in letting the law take its course. The lady wanted her husband dead. She got the job done. What difference does it make how she accomplished it?"

He was above it all, a little god with his angel a[t] his side and no dangers to concern him.

I looked at Ike, who met my eyes with the sam[e] expression I'd seen across a poker table when I wa[s] deciding whether to match his bet or fold. It was a[n] intimidating stare backed up by his hidden weapon[s] and naked nerve.

I butted out my smoke in an ashtray on the tabl[e] and slipped out of the booth.

"I'm going to talk with Lieutenant Baker," I tol[d] Ike. "You want to come along and sing your tun[e] with me, or would you rather solo when he sends fo[r] you?"

"I can wait."

"Okay," I said, looking at the other two, "bu[t] there's something else you folks should know. I'[m] expecting a call from Mr. Stucky this evening. H[e] wants to know who's got the necklace and he'[s] willing to pay for the information. Of course at thi[s] stage he doesn't really need anything too solid. Tha[t] means you three would be pretty good bets just as [a] matter of elimination. And Stuckey and his littl[e] brother don't worry a lot about proof or justice, jus[t] percentages."

For all the reaction that brought I might as wel[l] have said "Sweet dreams."

Two cops greeted me in the alley. They were bot[h] strangers, but the older one called me by name.

"Lieutenant Baker wants to see you."

"Dandy, I was just on my way to see him."

"Sure," said the cop politely and we got into thei[r] car.

Chapter 28

"So what'd you find out?" asked Lieutenant Baker.

"Your tails are getting better. I didn't spot them today."

"Didn't need any. Had men posted where I knew you'd go."

I thought about the room where Trixie was kept and tried imagining where they could listen. Probably just used a glass tumbler against the wall. I'd been stupid not to realize they'd be eavesdropping.

Baker watched me, looked smug as the goggle glasses would allow.

"If you know as much as God, why do you ask me questions?"

"I like to hear your whoppers. Who'd you find in Bitsy's kitchen?"

"You already know."

"That's right, so tell me what they said. You're ahead of me there."

"Ike admitted Trixie came to see him Friday

night—or Saturday morning. He even admits she brought him the necklace. She figured Bernie was going to give it to Adair and she went to Ike because he'd been her lover once and would hate Bernie for sleeping with his daughter. She was trying to get even with her husband, but I don't believe she thought Ike'd go over and kill him. Which is what I think he did. Maybe you can find somebody who saw him going to or coming from Bernie's place."

He slowly shook his head. "You're stretching, Wilcox. It comes down to her word against his, and we got all the proof against her."

"So you're not even going to pick him up?"

"Not while he's visiting the judge's girl friend, uh-uh."

"How about after?"

"You think it'll do me any good?"

"It won't do any damage."

"That depends on how buddy-buddy he is with the judge. The old man probably figures by now he can get that piece of jewelry real cheap. If he does, he won't want his salesman in trouble. He might talk too much."

"And what the judge wants, he gets, right?"

"You got a fine grasp on the facts of life, Wilcox."

That was nice. I didn't seem to have much hold on anything else. "I think the judge won't want the necklace any more," I said. "It's turned too hot and he's too smart."

"He's smart, all right. That's why he gets what he wants while pups like you just wag their tails."

"How about you? Are you getting what you want?"

His smile became blissful. "Of course, because I always want what the smart guys want."

I rolled a smoke and stared into the blankness of his thick lenses. He'd told me the philosophy of his life and it didn't shame him a particle. I supposed it was a lot more sensible than my absolute opposite twist.

"How do the smart guys want to settle things about the Podolack murder?" I asked.

"We'll settle that when we pick up your two sparring mates from the big city."

"You haven't had much luck with that so far."

"True." He didn't show much concern.

"They've already left town, probably. If they have, you'll never touch them."

"So you got a notion on how we can head them off, is that the verse I feel coming on?"

"They're going to call me. All I do is let them know who has the necklace. When they go after him, you've got them."

He took off his thick glasses and massaged the bridge of his nose gently with his right hand. He kept his eyes closed.

"All right," he said, putting the glasses back on. "When you get your call, let me know. If I'm not in, tell the sergeant."

"You still got Ike's house covered?"

"He never moves alone."

"Okay," I said, getting up. "I want to talk with Trixie again—if that's okay with the smart guys."

He waved his hand generously and I left.

I found Trixie stretched out on the cot, looking exhausted, as if her confessions had drained her like a session of diarrhea. Her eyes had the hopeless look of a sick pup. Slowly she sat up, adjusted her skirt and touched at her straggling hair.

"Where's Rita?" I asked.

"Gone back to the hotel."

"Okay, we seem to be getting somewhere," I lied. "Just hang on a while longer."

She nodded, found her purse beside the cot and dug out a comb which she pulled thoughtlessly through her hair. "Rita says when I get out of here, I can go back East with her."

"That sounds fine."

She gave up combing and rested her hands in her lap. "She's really a good kid, you know. We always got along. About all we ever had was each other. I mean, with Pa gone, there was only Ma and you couldn't talk over anything with her but mashed potatoes and the weather. Hated heat, couldn't stand cold."

I wondered where Rita got her brains. Maybe from grandparents or the old man. He'd been smart enough to duck out. Only more likely he'd just been shiftless like some others I'd known, present company included.

Trixie lifted her gaze to my face and brightened a little. "Rita thinks a lot of you, Carl. And I appreciate what you've tried to do. I know it's all my fault things are in such a mess, but we'll make it up to you. Rita's really stuck on you—she won't admit it, but believe me, I can tell. That's something when you stop to think of the guys she could have—really loaded ones who're crazy about her."

I wanted to swallow all that but wished she wouldn't press it so much. The hard sell always makes me uncomfortable.

"You know, this fella she has now," she went on, "he treats her like a queen, and in spite of that, she's not sure she wants to go back to him."

"I thought you just said you were planning to travel back with her."

"Oh, well, she'll have to go back East. That doesn't mean she's going to pick up where she left off. Hey, you travel a lot, why don't you come with us?"

"Sure. We can all travel in my Model-T coupe."

She laughed, stood up and kissed me on the cheek. "You get a bigger car and we'll work it out."

Rita had just washed her hair and met me at the door with her head wrapped in a towel.

"You look like a midget Punjab," I told her.

"A what?"

"That's a guy in Little Orphan Annie."

"I look like a *guy*?"

"The towel, it looks like a turban."

"That doesn't make me look like a guy," she said and moved against me. She was wearing a white silk robe.

"You sure don't *feel* like a guy," I admitted.

"How many guys have you felt?"

"Never touch them with anything but knuckles."

"Well, don't knuckle me."

"Never."

Soon she giggled and said my God you're eager and I said that was nothing to complain about or even laugh at and she said no, it was a great trait, don't ever give it up. As I carried her to the bed I decided if the phone rang we'd ignore it.

Nobody called. After the wrestle we stayed on the bed and I smoked while filling her in on my travels.

She listened quietly, took a deep breath when I was through and asked, "Are you really going to sic those men on old Ike?"

"You got another idea?"

"No, but I thought you liked him."

"I like him better than Baker or the hoods, but how else are we going to get Trixie loose?"

She propped herself up on one elbow and looked down at me. "I guess you're sorry you hired on, huh?"

I finished my smoke and butted it out in the ashtray on the bedside table.

"You figure you're being used, don't you?" she said.

I tried a shrug, but that's not much of a gesture when you're flat on your back.

She brought her face closer and I closed one eye to keep from looking cross-eyed at her nose. She gave me a warm kiss and drew away.

"Why'd Ike want to frame Trixie?" she asked. "Why'd he hate her?"

"I think it galled him that Trixie stayed with Bernie after she'd been to bed with Ike—and that Bernie wasn't jealous. Ike couldn't make Trixie that night because he despised her, not because he was too old to get it up. But the real ripper was Bernie treating Adair like a chippy. That turned Bernie and Trixie into a pair of cockroaches and she handed him the perfect chance to squash them both. Ike's all pride, you know? It's not enough you don't piss on him, you've got to know he goddamned *counts*. He could handle it fine if they hated him, but they ignored him and that did it."

I got up, dug my fixings out of my shirt and rolled a cigarette while Rita lay with her head propped up on both pillows. She pushed a loose strand of hair off her smooth forehead and blinked her blue eyes thoughtfully.

"The trouble," she said, "is that whatever happens with Ike when those men get to him, it'll still be easier for Baker to convict Trixie than to get all of what you're talking about straight. Even if things went so far that Ike confessed, wouldn't they still make her an accessory or something?"

"Probably not if the evidence she offered helped convict Ike."

I didn't spot any tail as we walked toward Fino's and I began wondering if Baker had decided to let Stuckey and Chuck have a free crack at me as well as Ike. The air was still, and the sun had dropped so low our long shadows stretched along the avenue ahead and up the walls. We saw only a couple other walkers and one car passed, a green Chevvie with dusty tires and dirty windows.

Fino's negro politely greeted us, and his dark bald head gleamed in the faint gaslight when he bowed. He led us to a corner table in a small room, lit the tall candles, promised a waiter, and faded away.

"Why do I keep expecting funeral music?" asked Rita.

I didn't know but felt the same way.

"Where is everybody?" she asked, looking around. "This place is like a tomb."

The waiter came in, looking like an undertaker in his black suit. His face was solemn.

"I'll have a French seventy-five," said Rita.

I ordered a beer.

The waiter spooked off.

"Make me laugh," she said.

"That guy looks like he'd only deliver hemlock."

"That's not funny," she said, but grinned a little.

I told her about the cross-eyed snake.

"Don't you know any long stories?"

"I only remember punch lines."

The waiter delivered our drinks in silence, and Rita took a swig of hers before the man had removed his hand from my stein.

"Don't get lost," she told him as he started off.

"You wish to order now?"

"No, but it won't be long."

He nodded coldly and was gone.

"A man like that," she told me, "would have to be a waiter to be missed."

"Relax."

"If I relax I may fall asleep. How come you always make me sleepy?"

"I don't know. Doesn't your keeper ever make you sleepy?"

"Don't call him my keeper. He's my friend. Tried and true."

"And generous?"

"That too. You can't shame me. I bet you'd like him. He's crusty as old Ike, but not as rough."

"Does he tell long stories?"

"No, he's not much for being funny. He watches me and laughs at things I say and gets a kick out of it when I tease him or tell him off. He's tired of fanny-kissers."

I wasn't too crazy about getting their cozy picture so I welcomed the glum waiter and ordered dinner plus another drink. Rita caught on and shut up about her friend.

We were just starting our second drinks when Big Tiny peered in from the hallway and smiled uncertainly. I waved him over.

He said he didn't want to intrude or anything, and I assured him he was welcome as a spring crocus so he pulled up a chair and the waiter took his order for alcohol and water.

He asked how I was doing.

"Ask me tomorrow."

He nodded gravely, glanced at Rita and said, "You get to see Trixie every day, don't you?"

She nodded.

"How's she holding up?"

"Okay, considering."

He nodded, turned his head to take in the deserted room, then bent forward as far as his paunch would allow. "I had a little talk with Lieutenant Baker this afternoon."

The waiter delivered his drink. Tiny thanked him politely and cradled the glass in his massive hands a moment.

We waited.

"He wanted to know if I'd seen Podolack after the poker session."

"You think you're a suspect?" I asked.

"Uh-huh. The lieutenant said I was big enough. I told him that was no kind of *reason*."

"Did he come up with one?"

"It's his notion I had some kind of deal with Ike."

He watched me as he lifted his glass and took a long drink. The glass thumped softly when he lowered it to the table. I could see he was working himself up to say something that worried him; he was agitated as a cow ready to deliver her calf.

"What's on your mind?" asked Rita in her soothing tone.

"Well, I hope you won't be upset about me saying it, but Ike and Trixie, they had sort of an affair a few years back."

"She already told me that," I said.

His half-hidden eyes came out to peer at me; I wasn't sure whether it was in surprise or shock, then he slumped back, rested his drink on his broad belly and stared at the glass as if he expected it to erupt with a genie offering magic wishes. Finally he lifted the glass, emptied it and called for the waiter, who appeared as if he'd been waiting outside the door. When the glass had been refilled, Tiny quickly took a deep swallow, wiped his mouth, and leaned across the table.

"The fact is, I watched Ike smother Bernie. Or finish it."

His eyes flickered from Rita to me.

"Careful," I said. "You're setting yourself up as an accessory."

He lifted his chins, said, "I don't care," and looked away.

"In stir the food's lousy. And no drinks. Once in a while somebody brews up something that'll get a few guys drunk, but about half the time it makes them blind too."

"Better me than Trixie." He eyed me squarely and I could see the martyr's mantle settling over his fat shoulders.

Rita leaned forward and put her small hand on his big paw. A moment later a tear rolled down the half acre of his cheek and jowl.

"You want to go over and get this on record at the police station tonight?" I asked.

He lifted his gaze from Rita's hand, blinked, squeezing out matching tears and shook his head.

"In the morning. I'll think about it till I got my story just right and I'm good and sober and then I'll tell them what I saw and they'll have to let Trixie go."

He left us when the waiter brought our supper, and before attacking her plate, Rita shook her head and said poor old Tiny, he'd become as big a liar as everybody else in town.

"You think it was drink that made him say that?" she asked.

"No. Pure sentiment."

"You think anybody'll believe him?"

"All it needs is one out of twelve on the jury. If

Howie does his job, I'd guess he could plant enough doubt to swing it."

Rita wanted to feel sorry for Tiny but couldn't help getting a boost from the notion that Trixie's chances had picked up, and she went after her meal with her usual ferocious efficiency.

I was rolling an after dinner smoke when the sour waiter came and said I was wanted on the telephone. Rita watched me get up, her blue eyes clear, excited, and confident. It seemed to me she should look a little worried, but all she showed was a lust for battle.

"Yeah?" I said into the black mouthpiece.

"Who did it?"

"Ike."

"Tell me about it," Stuckey said.

"When do I get my grand?"

"When you convince me."

"Like the whore said, I want my money while you're still hot."

"You don't trust me?"

"Damn right."

"Okay, I'll send a boy around with the grand."

"Nothing bigger than twenties."

"Any special serial numbers?"

"Nope."

"I thought you'd be reasonable. Okay, sit tight right there."

The minute he hung up I rang for the operator and gave her Ike's number. Adair answered on the first ring.

"Gimme Ike."

"He's asleep. Is this Carl?"

"Yeah, wake him."

"What's going on?"

"Stuckey and Chuck are on their way to talk to him."

"Oh, my God!"

"The house is covered by the cops. Lock the door and barricade your room in case they slip by. Tell Ike I'm on my way."

I streaked back to Rita, dropped a ten on the table and told her where I was going. She rose, saying she was coming with me, and since there was no time to argue I grabbed her hand and we took off.

The night was dark and still, filled with the sweet scent of alfalfa and the hum of crickets. I drove past Ike's house, looking for the stake-out and saw a car across the street that seemed occupied. There weren't any other cars along the dark street. I drove around the corner and parked by the alley.

"What're we going to do?" asked Rita as I hustled her toward the darkened house.

"I'm not sure. You still got the sock full of quarters?"

"Yes."

"Give it to me."

She did.

When I heard the beginning whine of the siren I thought it was the nine o'clock curfew; then realized that had sounded nearly an hour earlier. "Must be a fire," I said, and forgot about it as we approached the front door.

"What if those guys are already here?" whispered Rita.

"The cops would be out of their car across the street."

"If they *are* cops."

For some reason I wasn't shocked that she had no faith in Lieutenant Baker.

I tapped on the door. It opened and Ike said, "Come in."

We slipped past him into the dark hall.

"Where's Adair?" I asked.

"She's okay." For some reason that didn't reassure me.

"How long's that car been parked across the street?"

"Over an hour."

"Okay, it must be the cops and they're supposed to stay there unless they spot Stuckey and Chuck. There's probably another guy out back."

"So why're you here?" he asked.

My eyes were adjusting to the darkness, and I thought I saw a glint in his right hand.

"I told them you killed Bernie and probably took the necklace. It seemed only fair to come over and help you hold them off."

He went to the door and looked through the glass across its top. I joined him.

The siren rose to a peak once more and at the same time a dark car came smoothly down the street and halted beside the parked car. The driver got out, walked around the front, opened the right hand door of the parked car and a man inside came out with his hands raised. He was turned around, his hands came down, and a moment later he was shoved into the back seat. The second man emerged and went through the same procedure.

"What's going on?" demanded Rita.

"Stuckey just took care of the cops out front," I said.

"I don't suppose," said Ike calmly, "that whoever's posted out back can see what's going on out front?"

I supposed he was right because I figured they'd already been taken out.

251

"Rita," I said, "give the cops a call, will you? Where's the phone, Ike?"

"Never mind, we haven't got time for that."

He turned and lifted his hand so I could see the gun in the dim light.

"You two head back in the house. Move easy."

"What've you got in mind?"

"You're going in the basement, out of the way."

"Hey, Ike—"

"Move!"

The men outside had to be very near and his tone was so violent I knew he was ready to flip. I took Rita's arm and moved.

He hustled us to the rear vestibule and a moment later slammed the door and closed the bolt as we felt our way down the steps.

"What the hell does he think he's doing?" Rita asked.

"Must be planning to make a deal."

At the foot of the stairs I lit a match and looked around. A light cord hung almost directly before me and I tugged it, snapping on a dim bulb that showed us a cellar empty except for a coal furnace, a shovel, and two tubs filled with ashes and clinkers. The walkout, on the north wall, was secured with a padlock and the two small windows were boarded over. Apparently Ike had been expecting invaders.

The boarding up had been done hastily, leaving gaps. I grabbed the shovel and using its handle as a lever began prying one of the bottom boards loose. The nails were just beginning to give when I heard the first shot. I froze. Seconds passed. Then there were four rapid shots, louder than the first. I heaved on the shovel, the board came loose, and I started on the other. There was movement upstairs.

Rita brought me a hammer she'd found near the furnace and I used the claw pull on the second board, jerked it loose, knocked the glass out of the window, brushed aside slivers, and hauled myself up and out.

For a moment I crouched on the grass, breathing the fresh night air and listening. The siren had stopped. Overhead cottonwood leaves rustled while crickets chirped across the yard.

Pressing close to the south wall, I worked toward the front corner and peeked around. The porch was vacant. I thought I could hear a voice upstairs. A rustling behind me made me look back in time to see Rita wriggle through the basement window and scramble to her feet. I wondered what had made me think she'd stay quietly where she belonged.

She waved, ran lightly to the back corner and looked around it. Immediately she jerked back and signaled for me to come.

"What?" I whispered as I crouched by her side.

"Someone's out back, in the shed." She peeked again. "It's Chuck. He's got a ladder."

Since the shed was north of the house I figured he'd move back on that side. I grabbed Rita's hand and pulled her back to the front corner.

"Ike must've barricaded himself in the front bedroom. Stuckey's inside, trying to sweet talk him while brother Chuck plans to take him from the window over the porch. You stay by the front door and watch for Stuckey while I take Chuck, okay?"

She nodded.

I watched Chuck come around the corner, place the ladder against the porch roof and adjust it a couple of times, casual as a weekend painter getting ready for a job. Then he started up.

I snaked over the porch railing as his head moved out of sight. In three bounds I was across the porch, jumped to the opposite railing with one foot, slammed the other against the highest rung in reach and shoved.

He heard me coming and tried to scramble down as the ladder toppled outward. I heard his grunt, saw the gun in his hand, and then he yelled as he went over backward. The gun clattered on the ladder sidepiece and hit the ground before Chuck landed. I dropped to the lawn as Chuck shoved the ladder away, swung my cosh, missed his head and hit a ladder rung. Quarters exploded all over the yard.

Chuck roared, rolled to his feet and charged. I skipped aside, caught him with a right hook to the ear, and he bellowed, staggered and wheeled like a bull. I speared him with jabs, and hopped back over the ladder. He stumbled over it in pursuit and I brought my knee up, catching the top of his head instead of his chin, which hurt me more than it did him. The next time I dodged my knee gave, I staggered, tripped on the ladder and went down. The next second a ton of Chuck was on my chest, and his sausage fingers were digging for my throat. I snatched his little finger, but when it snapped all he did was bellow and squeeze harder. A roaring filled my ears, and when I tried to jerk my legs up to scissors him they only banged feebly on his half-acre back. Then he bucked, the hands jerked convulsively, he bucked again and fell forward. I wriggled free, tripped over that damned ladder again and sprawled in the grass. As I climbed to my feet I saw Rita busily swinging her purse at a round figure crawling toward her as she retreated.

I was pretty sore by then, maybe even unreasonable. I grabbed the ladder, told Rita to step aside, fitted the top rung under Chuck's chin, pulled the ladder over his back and sat down on the far end. He went limp on his belly with his face tipped toward the east and didn't make a sound.

"Where's Stuckey?" I asked.

"On the porch floor."

"Okay, take my place. I'll go check on him."

She said she thought Chuck was through, and I told her she hadn't been under him and I didn't think she'd ever want to be and without further debate she sat on the bottom rung.

I found Stuckey making crablike motions on the porch floor and realized just in time he was trying to reach the gun he'd dropped when Rita bopped him. I picked it up, dragged him to the steps and propped him against the left railing post.

He cautiously felt the top of his head, then slowly brought his hands down to his temples and held on, as if he thought his head would shatter unless he kept the pressure steady.

Suddenly he twitched, lowered his hands and peered around. "What'd you do to Chuck?"

"Don't ask. Can you stand?"

"Yeah, I think so."

I stood clear and kept the gun in plain view beyond his reach.

"Look to your left, in the yard."

It took a while before he could make it out and then he whispered, "Jesus."

Rita, apparently afraid the top ladder rung would strangle our pigeon, had stood up but kept both hands on the lower rung so she could push it down with full leverage of the ten-foot ladder if Chuck got ambitious. At the moment he wasn't in the mood.

"You've killed him," moaned Stuckey and he started to move past me. I tapped his beak with the gun muzzle, not too gently, and whoaed him pronto.

"Did you shoot Ike?" I asked.

255

"No, of course not."

"What were the four shots for?"

"He shot first. I had to impress him."

"So what happened?"

"He went up the stairs and barricaded himself in the front room. What'd you do to Chuck?"

"Knocked him off the ladder, punched him a little, kicked him once, and then Rita massaged his skull with her purse for a while. He's pretty docile right now, huh?"

"You've killed him. . . . He hasn't moved. . . ."

"That's right. It's the only way he can stay alive. If he tries anything he's had it. In about thirty seconds I figure he'll strangle if she lowers that end to the ground. So let's get down to cases; did you guys start the fire downtown?"

He closed his eyes, raised his hands to his head again, and said yes.

"Did you find a cop out back?"

"Yeah."

"What'd you do to him?"

"Gagged him. Handcuffed him to a tree."

"How'd you manage the guys out front?"

"Drove up beside them and stuck a gun through the window."

"Why'd you kill Podolack?"

"It was an accident. We were trying to find out if he had the necklace and he tried to outfox Chuck and Chuck held his head under water a little too long. Look, have her let up on that ladder, eh? He needs a doctor. . . ."

"I think you're right. If he wasn't in a bad way he'd roll over and start another frolic so you just keep talking and when we're squared away we'll see if somebody can put Humpty Dumpty back together again. Where'd you meet Bernie?"

"Chicago. At a poker game. I saw he was good and figured he was smart. I thought we could do business together."

"You work with the mob?"

"No, we've always been independent. Chuck lifts cars, I do jewelry. We were doing fine until some dumb flatfoot tried to collar Chuck and got himself killed. Everybody went crazy about that and we had to leave town and went to St. Paul. We didn't have good connections there for peddling stuff, but then I ran into Bernie at a speakeasy and he claimed to know everybody in South Dakota and said he could peddle anything we had. It worked fine for a while. Then I made a good hit in Minneapolis and when I delivered the stuff to Bernie he said he was short on cash, could I wait till he sold it. We hassled some, he gave me a couple centuries and I thought he'd be good for it. Then I heard he had this new girl friend and maybe was going to blow the territory so I got nervous and came back to collect."

"And he stalled you."

"I collected half. He promised the rest Sunday. I said if he didn't, we'd bury him."

"So where'd Podolack come in?" I asked.

"I didn't know anything about him till Bernie was dead. When I found out he was in the game, I checked with guys in the cities and they said he was here with some special merchandise for a hotshot. Then I knew Bernie'd planned to pull something and split, so we went to visit the frail."

"Adair."

"Yeah. Look, you've got the gun, have the lady ease up and call a doc okay?"

"When we're through. Were you guys watching Bernie's place that night?"

He nodded and stared glumly at Chuck.

"You saw everybody leave?"

"Yeah."

"Including Trixie?"

"That's right."

"What'd you do when she came out?"

"Had Chuck follow her."

He shifted his legs and I lifted the gun muzzle.

"Don't get any ideas, I may not be as tough as Rita, but like you said, I got the gun."

He hugged his knees and shook his head. "I'm not going to try anything. It's too late for anything but getting help for Chuck. He's all I got. . . ."

"So you sent him after Trixie. How long was it before Adair showed up?"

He lifted his head and let his chin sag. "How'd you know about that?"

"It just seemed likely. What happened?"

"Well, I'd gone inside to look around and found old Bernie spread out handier than fried chicken in the icebox, and just when I was set to ask him where he'd stashed his loot, I heard somebody come in the front door. I ducked down the hall and into the next room. Somebody came up the stairs and I heard a woman's voice and Bernie said something and then she said more and things got real quiet. I figured she was crawling in with him or untying him, you know, and then all of a sudden she was down the steps and gone. I went in the bedroom and found Bernie under the pillow."

"Didn't you hear any fuss while she was smothering him?"

"Well, I heard stuff, but I figured they were, you know, doing it."

"What'd you do after she left?"

"I looked around for the necklace and got out when I couldn't find anything."

"Where'd you think it was by then?"

"I figured Trixie had it when she left."

"Carl!" called Rita.

I stepped back from Stuckey and turned her way. She was waving toward the door behind me. I swung around and saw Ike, leaning against the door's edge. He had a gun in his hand, pointing at me.

"This son-of-a-bitch," said Ike, jerking his chin at Stuckey, "is a goddamned liar."

"So why are you pointing your gun at me?" I asked. Ike glared at Stuckey, but the gun kept pointing at me.

"Tell that woman to get the ladder off that gorilla," he said.

Rita looked at me and I nodded. She pushed the ladder clear and let it drop beside Chuck. Chuck slowly rolled over on his side and brought both hands to his throat.

"Go get him up," Ike told Stuckey. "Get him in your car and get the hell out of town."

Stuckey scrambled to his feet, stumbled off the steps, and trotted to his little brother. Slowly Chuck was coaxed up and they staggered off like two happy drunks heading home from a spree. A moment later they were gone.

"Now," said Ike, as Rita walked to my side, "just forget all that bullshit he told you. *I* killed Bernie. I did it because he was a son-of-a-bitch. You know it, and that's all anybody's got to know. You got your goddamned case solved. That's all that makes any difference, isn't it?"

"Sure. You want to lower the gun now?"

He stared down at it, shook his head and shoved the piece my way in his open hand. It was a little thing, just right for a lady's purse, very unlike Stuckey's cannon which had been in my hand while Ike was dictating. He'd never noticed.

Chapter 29

"Where's the god-damned necklace?" demanded Lieutenant Baker.

"Who cares? You got a confessed killer and two fugitives that admitted another killing with three witnesses who'll testify."

"Some witnesses. A confessed killer, an ex-con, and a professional madam."

"I'm no madam," said Rita. "I never ran a house in my life."

"So you're a single in the same business."

"You don't need the necklace," I said, trying to head off a blowup. "It doesn't figure in any of the killings."

"It sure as hell figured in Podolack's."

"Okay, you know that and we know it, but nobody else has to because you've got the jewels I handed over which'll take care of the motive just fine."

He grumbled and muttered and finally told us to get the hell out, and we left for the hotel where Trixie was relaxing with Howie. At least they were relaxing when Rita and I arrived. Rita had taken a suite with two bedrooms and the door was closed to the one Trixie was using.

We went to bed early but not to sleep. Later Rita came back from the bathroom and nudged me out of my doze.

"How come you haven't asked when we're leaving?"

"Haven't had time to think about it."

"Don't you give a damn?"

That came out a little stronger than seemed called for considering how cozy things had been earlier. I came to a little and reached up for her bare shoulder. She shrugged my hand off.

"It's just that you can't think ahead more than ten seconds, isn't it?" she said.

"You sound like you're looking for a fight. What'd I do?"

She sat back and shoved her hair off her forehead. "Don't you want to come back East with us?"

"Where you going to keep me when the man comes—under the bed?"

"Don't be ridiculous."

"I don't plan to. You can't keep me like a poodle."

"We could work something out if you really wanted to."

"Sure. What've you got in mind?"

"So I'm supposed to figure everything out, is that it?"

"It'd be a start. Right now I haven't got ambition enough for big plans."

"You never made a plan in your life. You just do what you want to do the minute you feel like it."

That was too true to argue and I didn't try. She stretched out, not quite making contact.

"Howie's going with us. He's really in love with Trixie."

"And she's crazy about him?"

"She appreciates him."

"She bringing along the quirt?"

She seemed to hold her breath and I expected an elbow in the ribs or worse, but then she giggled, rose up and leaned over me.

"You really *are* a bastard, you know that?"

"Only Ma knows for sure."

She took hold of my hair and rolled my head on the pillow.

"All right, so tonight's it. Let's not waste it."

In the morning she bought a new Buick and the three of them left early in the afternoon. Trixie kissed me good-bye, Howie gave me a two-handed shake, and Rita, who had turned cold with the sunrise, gave me an envelope.

"What's this?" I asked.

"Your pay-off."

"What for? You did all the work."

"I know. Just take it and we're square. No debts or regrets. We had a fine time, that's it. I don't want to drag it to death any more than you do. So long."

Howie returned by train a week later to handle Ike's defense. I didn't take in the trial, but Howie told me the old man went through it like a southern colonel being tried in a Yankee court. Howie spent all the time the judge would allow, telling the jury what a son-of-a-bitch Bernie had been and Trixie, who'd been called back for the show, gave enough details to sell the jury. They finally settled for involuntary manslaughter. What they wanted to do was give Ike a medal.

Nothing came up about the necklace and Adair was never mentioned. As far as I know, she's never been back in Aquatown.

A few weeks after the dust had settled I came across the judge and his lady in Fino's. She was wearing a low-necked green dress and an emerald necklace.

"Well," I said, pausing by their table, "I see everyone lived happily ever after."

The judge, looking whiter-haired and pinker-cheeked than ever, beamed and invited me to sit down and share a glass of champagne.

I said why not and asked what we were celebrating.

"A coming-out party," he said, grinning.

"How much did you pay?"

"What does it matter now?"

"It might tell me just how romantic you are."

"Hah!" said Bitsy. The judge gave her a quick glance, not quite as twinkly as usual, then turned back to me.

"I paid what would be sufficient to give the young lady a new beginning."

"So Adair could live happily ever after too, huh?"

The smile returned. "Even as we."

"Any notion where she went?"

"Not the slightest. Do you know now why she killed him?"

"The jury said Ike did it."

"Ike said Ike did it. You and I know better. The girl was the one. She was perceptive enough to know she couldn't keep him, so, like Porphyria's lover, she killed him to eternalize the moment. Have you read the poem?"

I raised my eyebrows.

"No, of course you wouldn't admit it if you had. It's a favorite of adolescents with precocious reading habits. The man strangled the young girl who came to his bed in the night, using her golden hair tangled around her delicate throat. And, speaking of romance, has your young lady friend departed?"

I nodded.

"Taking with her, I presume, the redoubtable Trixie. I'm surprised you didn't accompany them."

"So am I."

He laughed, waved the waiter over and had our glasses refilled. "I imagine the ladies were very grateful. Were the rewards generous?"

"Rita paid what she promised."

"With perhaps certain bonuses?"

"I figure you and your lady here made the most out of the whole business."

He looked at her and twinkled with satisfaction. "Yes, I think it's lovely how everything turned out. It's too bad the miscreants from the city escaped, but most of the errant citizens survived and the useless Bernie died at the hands of his mistress, which is probably the way he'd have preferred to go."

"Uh-huh. With no pain, eh, Judge?"

"Ah! So you have read the poem. But the other angle is, if you remember, Bernie appreciated pain."

He expected me to question that, and when I just drank my champagne and looked at him, he smiled some more.

"My friend," he said, "I'm afraid what you want is the last thing a wise man expects: justice."

Mostly what I expect is hypocrisy. I finished my drink, nodded at Bitsy and stood up.

"So long," I said. "See you in court."

"I shouldn't be at all surprised," he said.